Never Cross A Boss 5

Trust Issues Book 5

Tamicka Higgins

© 2017

Disclaimer

This book contains sexually explicit content that is intended for ADULTS ONLY (+18).

Chapter 1

Hakim could only be described as that one guy that nobody in the entire city would ever, in a million years, want to have a problem with. To say the least, when you have a problem with Hakim, you have a problem with your life. He was known in just about every part of Indianapolis. In so many ways, Hakim could be compared to that ever present fly on the wall that you want to get out of your house but can't for the life of you.

Hakim, who many people would say looked very similar to the rapper Method Man, especially back in his younger days, was approaching forty and still keeping up with his younger self. He rubbed his hands through Amber's thick hair, loving that he had found a black chick that had her real hair out. On top of that, she had lips that made his dick hard just by him looking at them. When he talked to the twenty-one-year-old, the way she licked her lips would drive him crazy. In his eyes, Amber looked like the kind of chick that took giving head seriously—treated it as if it were an art. Soon enough, he found out. And ever since, he has had her number saved in the contacts on his phone under a different name so that Tweety would not know it was her – so that she wouldn't know that he had a side chick.

Now that Tweety was out of the picture, Hakim enjoyed getting serviced by Amber's medium brown, thick self. Smiling, as his head had been bent back over the back of the couch, he looked down at Amber's thick body. Right then, Hakim shook his head. He reached down and slapped Amber's big ass, watching it jiggle as he pulled his hand away and placed it back on the dome of her head.

"Damn," Hakim said. "You got a fat ass, girl."

Amber, whose mouth was filled to the max with Hakim's manhood, giggled. She grabbed the base of his dick and pulled her head off, looking up and into Hakim's sexy, bugged-out eyes.

"You want some of this pussy?" she asked, already knowing that Hakim would. Hakim was an easy nigga, to her. He had money, looks, and was rough with her in a way that really turned her on.

Hakim nodded, hating how it felt when Amber lifted herself up off of his manhood. "Hell yeah," he answered. "Just suck on the dick a little while longer, okay? Damn, this shit feels good."

Amber smiled and giggled as she lowered her head back toward the head of Hakim's manhood. Never, for one second, did she break eye contact with Hakim. She could always tell how it drove Hakim so crazy to look dead into his eyes while she put work in on him. It turned her on to feel his big, bulky hands rub the top of her head – to feel his fingers rub through her hair. She knew that what really set her apart from other chicks in Indianapolis was the fact that not only was she pretty and could speak well with a body that most would pay for, but she also had real hair. Her hair was long – about down to her mid-back – black and thick. She used as few chemicals as she could in her hair and it showed in the classiest way. Her hair was obviously real and it was well taken care of. Men were drawn to this and their women were jealous. When Hakim would hit it from the back, lightly pulling Amber's thick hair was always the best leash, so to speak, that would keep Amber's body in place.

Hakim's head fell back onto the top of the couch as he enjoyed what he could only describe as a silk throat. Curse words slipped out of his mouth as he looked up at the white ceiling of his north side home, just off of Emerson. As one of Hakim's properties, this was probably the most homely with the best location. Located in a fairly stable area, the streets were windy and had tall trees rising toward the sky on both sides, hugging the pavement. Back up off of the streets were houses on slight slopes that allowed the garages to be basement garages. Hakim's eyes scanned the all-white front room of his house, fish tank and all, before looking down at Amber and the work she was putting in on his dick. He let out a grunt just as he noticed that his phone was vibrating in his coat pocket. He reached over to his coat, which was hanging over the right arm of the couch, and fished out his phone. Upon looking at the number, seeing that it was his boys Raul and Jayrone, he felt no need to tell Amber to stop what she was doing.

"Yeah?" Hakim answered the phone. "Wassup?"

"We out at the gate," Raul said, his Puerto Rican accent coming through strong over the phone. "You got the gate closed and we can't pull up in here, Hakim."

"Fuck," Hakim said, not wanting to pull Amber's head off his manhood. Reluctantly, he gently grabbed Amber's chin and lifted her up, loving how she had even kept her tongue moving the entire couple of seconds he took to pull her head up. He walked over to the window, looking out at the driveway, and saw that indeed Raul and Jayrone were sitting, in their black car, just outside of the gate.

After letting the blinds close, Hakim walked over to the kitchen where he pressed a button to open the gate. "It's open," he said into the phone, talking to Raul. "Come on up. I'll have the door open. I got a little chick over here, but you already know."

A chuckle came through the phone. "Yeah," Raul said then hung up.

Quickly, Hakim went back over to the couch. Immediately, Amber's hands began rubbing his thick, somewhat muscular body through his white long sleeve shirt as he let go of his pants. They fell back to the floor around his ankles as he leaned back on the couch. "Keep suckin' that dick, okay?" Hakim said. "I'm bout to have a couple niggas over, if that's cool."

Amber shrugged. "Okay," she said. "That don't mean I'mma stop doin' what I'm doin' just cause they here."

Hakim smiled and nodded his head. "Yeah," he said. "That's that shit a nigga like." He put his hand back on the top of her hand. "Go on and do what you do, okay. Maybe we go out to eat or somethin' later on, okay."

Amber smiled, nodded her head, then went back to giving Hakim just what he needed the most. Within a couple of minutes, there was a tap at the front door. "It's open!" Hakim announced.

Raul and Jayrone stepped into the house, closing the door behind them. Raul was tall and clearly of Puerto Rican descent, as his skin was brown and his hair was jet black. Jayrone, on the other hand, was clearly black, with a skin color that made him look as if he had been out in the sun. His bushy eyebrows and goatee made him handsome, in his own way, as he clearly looked like a dude from the street.

It did not take either of them long to see that Hakim was sitting on the couch, his legs spread, with a fat-assed chick on her knees. She was kneeled over and giving Hakim what looked like some professional head. Both Jayrone and Raul tried to not think about how good this chick's mouth must have felt, let alone how her pussy would feel while looking down at her big brown ass clapping. They knew that the main reason they were even over here was to talk to Hakim about the very nigga – Marcus – who had fucked around with his chick Tweety. Never, especially now, would they think of trying to drop their dick into a chick that had Hakim's attention. They both cared too much about their lives to ever make a mistake like that. It did not matter how good the chick looked, she was simply off limits.

Hakim looked at Raul and Jayrone and smiled. "Wassup my niggas?" he said, looking at them as if he wanted to know why they looked so surprised by what they were seeing. "Damn, you ain't gon' say wassup to a nigga?" he said then chuckled.

Instantly, Raul leaned over Amber and shook Hakim's hand, looking down at Amber's head rising up and down in Hakim's lap. Jayrone then did the same, but really having to watch himself with how hard he glanced down at Amber.

When Raul and Jayrone backed away from Hakim sitting on the couch, they plopped down into the couch on the other side of the room, sliding out of their coats.

"So," Hakim said. "Wassup?" He motioned toward Amber. "A nigga only got a few more minutes with her so just talk to me till I'm done."

Feeling a little awkward that they were going to hold a little conversation with Hakim while he was getting head, Raul went on and dove right in to what they came to say.

"Yeah, yeah," he said. "So, Hakim, we can't find this nigga nowhere."

Hakim allowed Amber's silky throat to keep him calm. While thinking about what he had just been told, he gently pushed Amber's head down further. Hearing a woman gag on his meat was one of Hakim's favorite sounds in the world. It was also something he liked to feel when he was feeling a little aggressive, like right now, as he did not like how this nigga, Marcus, was taking up so much of his time and effort. Yet, he was not going to just throw the towel in and give up on looking for him. He knew that when he found Marcus—and he was going to find him, no matter what, he'd tie him to his pool table down in the basement and show him what another man gets when he messes with the wrong dude's chick.

"Man," Hakim said, now looking across at Raul and Jayrone. "Where all y'all look for the nigga? This shit is takin' too much of my fuckin time, for real though. Where all did y'all look for this nigga?"

Jayrone and Raul looked at one another then back to Hakim.

"Well," Jayrone said, clearly sounding as he was from Baltimore or somewhere like that. "We told you about what happened at the girlfriend's house, Hakim," he said. "I can't believe we ain't get his ass when he went over to his place and put all them bullets into it. I mean, fuck, Hakim, we really shot that shit up. Busted windows and blew holes in doors and shit."

"Whatever, whatever," Hakim said, the sounds of Amber's mouth filling the room like background noise. "I'm passed that shit, ya feel me? What else? Tell me some shit that I ain't heard yet."

"A'ight then," Jayrone said. "So, last night, when we left the house over on Paris, the girlfriend's house, she had told us that that nigga Marcus was still down in the hospital. We went there and shit, to the room that she said, and found some old white lady laying there. Man, I was fuckin' shitty about that shit, my nigga."

"What the fuck you expect?" Hakim asked. "You thought that she was gon' send y'all niggas to the right place when she really ain't have to. Damn, I think y'all niggas stupid."

Hakim looked down at Amber, hearing her giggle at how he owned these two grown men as if they were little boys. He smiled at her, rubbing the top of her head as she continued on with what she was doing, not even coming up for air or because her jaw was tired and numb.

"Yeah," Raul said. "Well, we told the little bitch that if she was lyin' to us, then we would be back. She got a body that I could smash real fuckin' good."

"Oh yeah?" Hakim said, his eyebrows rising. "Is that so?"

Just then, Amber pulled her head up and looked at Hakim as if she has just caught an attitude. Hakim chuckled a little and looked down at her. "What's that got to do with you?" he asked Amber, sounding very authoritative. Before Amber could even think of something to respond with, she felt her head being pushed back down.

"So then what?" Hakim asked.

"Well," Jayrone said, continuing. "After we ain't find him there, at the hospital, we went back up to the house."

"And, let me guess," Hakim said. "The girlfriend and her family was gone, right?"

Jayrone and Raul looked at one another, knowing that neither of them wanted to answer Hakim's question. They both then looked back at Hakim and nodded.

Hakim put his head back, feeling the dome at the back press against the back of the couch in frustration. If Amber was not in front of him right then, on her knees and sucking his dick like it was her last meal, Hakim would have jumped right up at this point and been across the room, slapping the shit out of Jayrone and Raul. He looked at both of them, wanting to tell them how lucky they were that Amber was there and that he didn't want to be rude.

When he looked back down at Jayrone and Raul, he shook his head. "A'ight," he said. "So, then what? Where the fuck y'all niggas been at today that y'all just now gettin' here to tell me this shit?"

"We was sittin' over outside the girlfriend's house on Paris," Raul said. "Right by the highway and shit, waitin' on her to come back, if they came back. We sat over there off and on and ain't never seen nothin'. So, if they did come back, they did it when we wasn't there. Hakim, we gotta figure out where else to look for this dude. We been at the girlfriend's house and back at the nigga's apartment and shit, and it's like they done disappeared. We had to get a little rough with this scrawny little white doctor dude at the hospital to give us any kind of address, but the address they had, which the dude said was Marcus' mother, once again, had some fuckin' white people at it when we drove by and parked by it and shit. I don't think that she live there no more."

Hakim nodded, processing what they were saying to him. With all of the money he lost because of Marcus, and finding out that he had been in Tweety while he was out of town, Marcus stayed at the back of his mind at all times and only motivated him to keep looking. Hakim looked down at Amber. He gently placed his hand under her chin and lifted her head up off of him. His dick jumped when he looked into Amber's eyes. However, this time, Hakim's eyes were somewhat cold.

"Go make the three of us somethin' to eat, would you?" Hakim said to Amber. "This is serious, baby. We gotta talk about some real shit."

Amber did not object. Instead, she kissed Hakim's dick before pressing into his thighs to stand up. She looked back at Raul and Jayrone, looking them both in the eyes. She smiled and licked her lips as she always did as she walked away. Neither Jayrone or Raul realized that their eyes were following the plump backside of Amber as she walked out of the room and headed toward the kitchen.

"What the fuck y'all niggas lookin' at?" Hakim asked, his voice sounding thunderous to Raul and Jayrone, as they had been practically hypnotized by how Amber's cheeks bounced when she walked.

Without a second through, Raul and Jayrone both focused their attention on Hakim. He was pulling his pants up and fastening his belt buckle.

"What else we know about this dude?" Hakim asked. "I talked to the nigga that hooked me up with the nigga and he said that his boys been over, but he don't know where they live or nothin'. If he did, he woulda told me, and we'd be goin' over to see them and shit. Apparently, Marcus got two little niggas that he basically best friends with and shit, but I don't know 'em, so that stops right there."

Raul shrugged his shoulders. He'd only been in Indianapolis for about a year, having come up with some of his cousins who knew Hakim and got him in contact with him. After living in Miami for the better part of his life, he had become an expert in basically helping people – people like Hakim – find somebody. Typically, it was him looking for somebody because they owned someone money. However, as he got older, he branched out to even finding a side chick for a wealthy wife of a drug lord in Columbus, Ohio. However, things were a little different for him in Indianapolis because he still was not totally connected with the social networks in the city, and the culture was so much different than Miami's that keeping an ear to the street was proving to be a little difficult for him.

Raul's ignorance for once gave Jayrone the upper hand. As Raul was typically the driver, and the one who arranged a lot of stuff, Jayrone always felt like somewhat of a side kick to Raul. At times, it was okay and was something that he could live with. However, there were other times that he felt like Raul was sonning him. Moments like these helped to even the score because Jayrone, even though he was from Baltimore, had been in Indianapolis for far longer and knew quite a few people.

This helped him to be the one to lead the way on them finding out more about Marcus.

"I hit a cousin up," Jayrone said, sounding confident. "And I asked him if he knew Marcus. We ain't have his last name, as you know, at that time, but when I described him and what his girlfriend look like, he said he knew who the fuck I was talkin' bout."

"Word?" Hakim said. "Is that right?"

Jayrone nodded. "Yeah, man," he said. "And he friends and shit with some older niggas up and around the city and shit. And he said that he know Marcus from bein' over this nigga Roy's house, somewhere over on the west side."

"Roy?" Hakim asked. The name sounded so very familiar, as his boy George had gotten him into contact with a Roy. Hakim had hit him up and was now waiting on the dude to respond. "Roy what?"

"I don't know," Jayrone answered, shaking his head. "All I know is that my cousin was over his place, somewhere on the west side, and said that he think the nigga Roy is Marcus's uncle and shit."

Hakim nodded, smiling. "Is that right?" he asked. "This nigga Roy might be Marcus's uncle, huh?"

Hakim thought about how coincidental it was that this dude Roy would be hitting him up just when he was basically scouring the city looking for Marcus – looking for the very person that might be his nephew. Hakim glanced at his phone, which was sitting on the couch next to him. George had said that Roy wanted to talk to him about some business and about catching up from back in the day, but Roy had never really had all that much of a relationship that would be worth either of them trying to catch up. Nonetheless, as Hakim has gotten older, he'd become a little more sociable than he had been at one point. Rather than closing doors the way he used to, he'd crack them and see if whoever was trying to come in would be worth it.

"You know the dude?" Raul asked, noticing how Hakim was rather stuck on the name Roy. "Hakim, man? You know him?"

Hakim nodded. "I might," he said then looked back at Jayrone. "And you said that he might be this nigga's uncle?"

Jayrone nodded. "That's what he said."

Hakim nodded. "Well," he said. "Ain't this some shit."

"And what some shit?" Jayrone asked.

Just then, Amber came walking back into the living room. Instantly, Jayrone and Raul looked at her thick brown body. They both took quick glances before looking away, not wanting Hakim to dare see them looking too hard in Amber's direction. Amber, walking up as if she knew she was the baddest chick in the entire zip code, smiled at the three men.

"Excuse me," she said. "Hakim, baby, you ain't got much for a bitch to work with in this kitchen. What you want me to make with the slim pickings you got to work with in the fridge? Don't even get me started on what's in them cabinets."

Hakim looked across at Raul then Jayrone, knowing that he needed to talk to them on a serious note at this point. He did not have time to be dealing with simple bitches that came interrupting his conversation with stupid questions – questions for which they should knew the answer because it is so obvious.

Hakim looked at Amber and stood up. Quickly, he reached out and slapped her ass, smiling as he felt it jiggle under the weight of his hand. Raul and Jayrone both jumped for a split second, Hakim's contact sounding as if it could hurt Amber. They each tried to keep from grinning and saying damn.

"You know what you need to do for a nigga," Hakim told her. He went to his bedroom and came back with a few hundred dollar bills. He handed them to Amber. "Go get a nigga some groceries and shit so he ain't gotta starve and shit. Get whatever you want and shit and by the time you get back, we'll be good and hungry. Then, later on, maybe we can hit the mall up or something."

Amber smiled, loving how Hakim just took charge of her. He was the realest nigga that she had ever had. And he always knew just what to say to get her attention, remembering that her taste in the finer things in life was something she longed for just about every day of the week. She grabbed the money, then Hakim kissed her, slapping her ass again, causing her to scurry back to the bedroom and get into some clothes. Within a matter of minutes, Amber was dressed and the three men watched as her thick body bounced out of the side door and onto the driveway.

Hakim looked at Raul and Jayrone and smiled. "That's my new chick," he said. "The bitch's name is Amber and, as you can see, she got an ass that just won't quit, and a throat that just won't stop soakin'."

"Damn," Jayrone said, shaking his head. "That's wassup."

Just then, Hakim walked away and into the dining room. In seconds, he had returned and was now sitting on the couch as he rolled a blunt. "A nigga gon roll this shit up and we can stand out back and smoke while I let Roxy out. She ain't be out today, yet."

Roxy was Hakim's Pit Bull, who had her own area downstairs, next to the garage. Hakim had had the dog for some years, and liked how she was aggressive when she needed to be but friendly when all the aggression was not necessary. Hakim finished rolling a blunt then led Raul and Jayrone down the basement steps. Within minutes, the three dudes stood side by side out on the patio that let out from the basement and looked out at a large, snow-covered yard. Wooded land set at the back of the property, the bare trees acting like a wall to the other side – whatever was on the other side.

Hakim passed the blunt around, loving how it felt to smoke some good shit when it was cold outside. "Niggas," he said. "I been thinkin' bout this shit since we came out here and shit."

"What?" Raul asked, wanting clarification.

"The nigga Roy," Hakim said, as if the answer should be obvious. "The nigga you was just tellin' me about. I used to know that nigga back in the day, sort of, when we was young and shit. Never really knew him personally or nothin', but we hung in some of the same circles. Paths crossed in some of the same hoods and shit, you know? The funny thing is, though, that I'm waitin' on his ass to hit me back up."

"Word?" Jayrone said, finding it funny as well.

"Yeah," Hakim said. "He hit me up about try'na do some business or somethin', through a nigga we both know and shit. I hit him up and he ain't returned my call yet."

Hakim checked his phone again as they all stood there.

"Damn," Raul said. "Ain't that some shit."

"Right," Hakim said, smiling. "A real fuckin' coincidence."

"You don't think he know you after his nephew, do you?" Jayrone asked.

Hakim shrugged. "I don't know what I know," he answered. "What do I think? I think the nigga do probably know. But, fuck, I don't know if he close to his nephew like that. We can't even find the nigga and don't know who he might be tellin' what. Word was that his boys, the little niggas I told y'all about in the living room, ain't even know that he was caught up in no shit. So, that tell me that he prolly ain't talkin' as much as we think. But then again, I don't really know."

"Bet," Jayrone said. "I think it is the nigga's uncle. I mean, what are the fuckin' coincidences. This shit sound like some shit where he know why he hittin' you up, but he really don't wanna say."

"Yeah," Raul said, agreeing with Jayrone. "Hakim, man, you really think that you gon' meet up with him and shit?"

"That's what I been thinkin' about," Hakim said. "At first, I was cool with it and shit. Didn't even think anything of it. Now? Now, I'm thinkin' about what this nigga's real intentions could be. You can't trust nobody out here, especially not nowadays. I don't give a fuck who they is. I'mma play it cool and shit and be friendly and all that with the nigga, but we gotta be ready for his ass."

"Ready?" Raul asked, nodding his head. "I like that shit."

"Yeah," Jayrone said. "That's smart, that's smart. Be ready for his ass, just in case he do know some shit."

"And if he don't, no love lost," Hakim said. "We gon' be ready for the nigga, so that even if he is here on some real shit and not because of his nephew, then we can at least get something out of him – see where the nigga go when he leave here and shit, even if it is home."

The three of them nodded their heads as they watched Roxy sniff around Hakim's vast backyard. At this point, it was only a matter of time before Roy would be hitting Hakim up to return his call. All the while the three of them talked about what actions they would take, Hakim was thinking about what he would say to Roy. He was going to play his cards close to his chest, so to speak, with this little meeting. And, no matter what, he was not going to come out losing.

Chapter 2

Roy had spent some time smashing Cherry, putting all he had into it like it was his first time getting inside of that pussy. She did her usual, showing him that he was still the man. She screamed, she squealed. She got down on her knees and pleased the dick like a man needs it to be pleased. After he got done really giving it to her, they smoked and went on with their day. Once Roy had left the bedroom to go out to the living room, he saw that Hakim had hit him back. Quickly, the situation at hand, which had never left his mind, was front and center. He reminded himself that he needed to call Lorna when he got done talking with Hakim, and that he would probably go over to her house later on tonight to see how she was doing.

Roy called Hakim back. On the third ring, Hakim answered. The sound of a dog barking was in the distance. "Yeah," Hakim said. "Wassup?"

Roy, standing in his underwear in the middle of his living room floor, turned toward the front window of his house and looked out at the street. He could have given two fucks about anyone looking in as they rode by his house, as his blinds were open. Even at his age, he knew he had nothing to be ashamed of below the belt.

"Wassup, Hakim," Roy said, quickly thinking of what direction he wanted to take the conversation. "This Roy, my nigga. How you been, bruh?"

"I been good, I been good," Hakim said.

Roy could hear the coldness in Hakim's voice. It was obvious that the man was trying to hide his frustration. Roy knew he'd have to tread carefully with this conversation.

"Wassup, nigga?" Hakim asked. "Long time no see."

"Man, nothin'," Roy answered. "A nigga just been busy and shit, you know how it be."

"You still out in these streets?" Hakim asked. "You still doin' that shit?"

"Fuck yeah," Roy answered. "That's actually why I'm callin' you, Hakim, as a matter of a fact."

"Oh yeah?" Hakim said.

Roy explained to Hakim that he wanted to meet up with him and talk about something to do with moving some work. He lied and said that the word around town was that Hakim was that nigga everyone wanted to talk to when it came to the distribution aspects. In fact, Roy even went so far as telling Hakim that he was interested in talking with him about moving some stuff from other states and that people had said he was the best person around to talk to about that.

Hakim continued on the conversation with Roy, the two of them agreeing to Roy coming through his house later on, in a couple of hours. Roy liked the time, as it would give him enough time to hit his sister Lorna up and see if she had made it back from Fort Wayne all right.

"A'ight then," Hakim said. "Just hit me up when you pull up at the gate and I'll let you in." He gave Roy his address. "And we can chill and smoke and shit while we talk, if you cool with that, nigga?"

"Hell yeah," Roy said, trying to sound as friendly as possible. "I'm down with that."

When Roy hung up, he stood for a moment frozen in his living room floor. He was going to meet with Hakim in about a couple of hours. There was an uneasy feeling about him that he had not anticipated having when he had first hit up Hakim. There was something about Hakim's voice that not only sounded uneasy but also came across as skeptical. Roy tried to shake it off as he called Lorna.

"Hello?" Lorna answered.

"Wassup, Sis?" Roy said. "You back from up north or what?"

Lorna sighed. "Just got in the door as a matter of a fact," she answered. "About to take them clothes and shoes off and lay my ass down for a minute. I prolly won't go to sleep or nothin', but I just need to lay down for a minute."

"Was Larry cool and everything?" Roy asked. "I ain't seen the nigga in a minute."

"Yeah," Lorna said. "He cool. I made sure to tell Marcus that he better respect that it's Larry's house and not to go getting involved in anything that is only going to make his situation even worse than it already is. You ain't talked to him, have you?"

"Now, Lorna," Roy said. "You told me you ain't want me talkin' to him no more."

Roy was lying. Marcus had hit him up since being dropped off in Fort Wayne to see what his uncle was out there doing for him. Roy gave him a quick rundown of what he knew and what was going on, like him waiting on Hakim to hit him back up. However, he made a deal with his nephew to never tell his mother that the two of them had talked. They both needed to keep the same story going, so it only made sense that Roy would tell him to never tell his mother that the two of them had spoken.

"Okay," Lorna said, glad that her brother had not betrayed her trust by talking to her son. She loved her brother as much as she always had, but with driving back from Fort Wayne, she had a lot of time to think. This time helped her realize even more that Roy was truly responsible for ushering Marcus into this life where he now had to hide out two hours and some change away from Indianapolis.

"I was callin' to tell you that I'm goin' to meet with Hakim, Lorna," Roy said. "I'm goin' in a couple of hours."

There was a brief pause on the phone before Lorna spoke. "Is that right?" she asked. "Roy, don't go makin' this bigger than it really is. You don't think that this Hakim nigga or whatever his name is will just go on somewhere after not bein' able to find Marcus?"

Roy knew what his sister was trying to do, but she had no real sense of just how deep Hakim's reach, so to speak, went in this city. Furthermore, he was not the kind of man who was going to stop looking because things got a little hard.

"Lorna," Roy said, sounding sterner. "I really don't think that he is just going to give up. Like I told you, I ain't seen the dude in some years, but he ain't strike me as the kinda guy who is just gon' give up."

"Well, what you gon' talk about when you go over there later on, Roy?" Lorna asked.

"Lorna, calm down," Roy said. "He don't even know why I'm really goin' over there. As far as I know, he don't even know that me and Marcus is related. At least, I don't think he know that shit. He think I'm just comin' over there to talk about some business and shit, you know, but I'mma see what kinda shit he say that might tell me what this nigga is really thinkin'. If nothin' else, we'll know where to find the nigga."

"Find him?" Lorna said, as if she didn't understand. "What you mean find him? Roy, you betta not. You not thinkin' about trying to retaliate and shit, are you?"

Lorna could hear her brother's silence. Silence, for Roy, had never meant anything good. This was even the case back in the day, back when they were teenagers. "Roy?" Lorna yelled into the phone.

"Look, Lorna," Roy said. "I ain't try'na have it come to that. Like I said, I'mma just go over there and talk to him. Maybe work my way around to bringin' the shit up, but I still don't know what I'mma do."

"Oh God," Lorna said. "Okay, okay. Whatever. Just be careful when you go over there, Roy. Just be careful."

"Don't you worry, Lorna," Roy said. "You just worry about yourself and Marcus. I don't know who this is that Hakim might got ridin' around the city doin' his dirty work and shit for him, but I don't want them to find out where you live and shit and be bustin' through your door."

"I wish them niggas would," Lorna said, sounding tough. "Let'em run up in here and I'mma shoot'em."

"Yeah," Roy said. "Just watch out and shit with what you doin' and when you go places. I don't really know how these niggas found out that Marcus's little girlfriend stay over on Paris. I don't know who Hakim know, but I doubt he know that I'm Marcus's uncle."

"Yeah, yeah," Lorna said. "Just don't do no shit that is going to get you killed."

"Okay," Roy said. "I'mma go on and get ready so I can head out in a little bit and get over there. You want me to stop through when I leave his place? I can bring you something to eat."

"It's whatever," Lorna said.

On that note, Roy ended his phone conversation with his sister. He went back to his bedroom, picking out something to wear – black jeans and a long-sleeve black Polo shirt – before taking a shower. Before walking out of the door, he grabbed himself something to eat. In so many ways, he hated to admit that he was a little nervous at the idea of going to meet with Hakim. At the same time, however, he was going to do whatever it took to make sure that Hakim did not get to his nephew…even if it meant taking Hakim out first.

***

When Lorna hung up the phone from talking to her brother, she went to her bed and lay down for a minute. After she'd drifted off to sleep for about forty-five minutes or so, she woke up to her phone vibrating. It was her friend, Sheena. She answered, glad that she could have a chance to talk to a familiar voice that was just real people. Before leaving Fort Wayne, Lorna had sent a text message to Sheena, saying that she would need a ride over to Marcus' apartment to get his car. His keys were in Lorna's purse.

"Hello?" Lorna answered.

"Girl," Sheena said. "I am just now getting off work and I seen your text message. Did you still need a ride to get Marcus' car?"

"Yeah, I do," Lorna told her. "Whenever you can come," she said, being considerate. "No rush or whatever."

"Girl, I can come on over there now," Sheena said. "What's wrong with Marcus's car, anyway? Why you got to go get it?"

Lorna had not told Sheena, who was her best friend, anything about what all happened with Marcus. In so many ways, Sheena was like a sister to Lorna. However, throughout her life, Lorna had learned that there were times when she couldn't even trust her very best of friends. She just wished that Marcus would learn the same thing before he got into even more trouble down the road.

"Long story, girl," Lorna said, trying to buy time. "How soon you think that you can be over here and I can be ready?"

"I be there in twenty, thirty minutes," Sheena said.

Lorna hung up and got back to her feet, heading out in the living room. In what seemed like only fifteen minutes, Sheena was knocking at the door. When Lorna let her in, she looked at her, shaking her head. "Girl, where the hell you comin' from?" she asked.

Sheena was pretty, in her own way. To a lot of people, especially the younger kids, she looked like a heavier version of the singer Keyshia Cole. Everything about her had a California look to it, even though she was from southern Indiana, a small city called Evansville. Sheena strutted into the living room, leopard pants hugging her waist, her belly button showing, and a white button-up shirt looking as if it were about to burst at the seams from how large of a chest she had.

"Girl, you know I gotta look good all the time," Sheena said, confidently. "Come on so I can get you over to Shadeland and shit. I met this nigga I'm hangin' out with a little bit, but I gotta wait for him to get off work."

"Girl, you somethin' else," Lorna said, shaking her head. Sheena was everything that she wanted Marcus to not bring home. During the day, she worked hard and was very professional as a secretary at a law firm for a bunch of white men downtown. However, as soon as she hit the pavement outside of the office building at 5:01 p.m., Sheena turned into the most ghetto queen, making sure that she was always wearing the tightest pants – doing the most to make sure that any man walking by would notice her butt. Lorna slid into her coat and they headed out the door. "I'm ready, I'm ready."

Lorna climbed into the front passenger side seat of Sheena's modest red Saturn, and Sheena backed out of her driveway and headed toward the main road.

"So, what is wrong with Marcus's car that you would need me to help you go get it to bring it back to your place?" Sheena asked, really wanting to know.

Lorna thought. *Damn, this bitch is like a dog with a bone. I should have known that she wasn't going to just come pick me up and take me. She would have to ask the twenty-one questions. And I would have to come up with the twenty-one answers. No matter what, I ain't telling her what happened with Marcus. The kind of niggas she hung out with could be the very ones who are hooked up with this Hakim nigga.*

Lorna looked over at Sheena. "Awe, girl," she said. "It's nothing serious or anything like that. Marcus just went outta town for a minute to see some of our family." She then added "down south" to throw Sheena off, in case that information got out and into the wrong hands. "He just didn't want his car sittin' over at his apartment, unmoved, for too long. You know how they stealin' cars left and ride in Indianapolis nowadays, girl."

Sheena zigzagged through the city's east side. "Yeah, girl," she said. "You right about that. Well, it's good that he get to go the hell outta here and go somewhere. And shit here right now, no way, but a bunch of snow and ice. He betta off down south for a minute, if he can get away from what he doin' and enjoy it."

For the rest of the fifteen minute or so ride over to Marcus' apartment complex, Lorna purposely steered the conversation in other directions. They talked about a new store opening in the mall downtown, the next weather front, the new music from the younger people that they heard on the radio, and some other easy gossip. Before Lorna knew it, Sheena was pulling her car through the check-in gate at Marcus' apartment complex, then into a parking spot just in front of Marcus' apartment. It didn't take Sheena long to notice that one apartment – just one of many – was boarded up. It was obvious to her that something had gone down here.

"Damn, what happened over there?" she asked. "Wait a minute, ain't that Marcus's apartment building, Lorna?"

Lorna shook her head as she was undoing her seatbelt. "Naw, girl," she answered, lying. "Marcus told me that that apartment was some niggas or something and the place had a little fire. But, don't worry, they was able to contain it and whatnot. Marcus actually lives across the hall. One of the reasons he went ahead and took his trip down south now was because the apartment owners had to do some repainting and so it just worked out that way."

"Oh, okay," Sheena said, not entirely sure if she believed the story Lorna had just fed to her.

On the other hand, Lorna was happy that she was able to come up with something so quickly to answer Sheena's question. Whether or not Sheena bought what she'd said wasn't important. Lorna thanked her friend for bringing her to Marcus' apartment, even going as far as to offer some gas money. Sheena declined her offer and told her that she would text her later on, after hanging out with the new guy she'd met. As Sheena pulled off, she yelled through the window, telling Lorna to not wait up if she didn't hear from her.

Lorna climbed in behind the wheel of Marcus' car and turned the engine over. She sat for several minutes, allowing the car to warm up. All the while she sat there, she could not help but keep her eyes fixated on what had been Marcus' apartment. The image of bullets nearly missing Marcus' head flashed in her mind. After just a few seconds of those, Lorna went ahead and put the car into DRIVE.

Lorna drove all the way home, feeling that odd feeling that comes from driving an unfamiliar car. On the way there, she turned into 102.3 and listened to some old school R&B that was out when she was in high school. Lil' Mo's *Superwoman*, with Fabolous, played, taking Lorna back. Then, Mystikal's *Danger* came on, which was out when Lorna was in middle school.

Upon turning into her driveway and parking, Lorna had used her automatic garage door opener to raise the garage door. Once opened, she could see that she was going to have to clean the garage out before she could even think about putting Marcus' car inside of it. She hadn't realized just how much stuff she had continuously crammed into it over the years. She shook her head, the curse word *fuck* slipping out of her mouth. Lorna left Marcus' car in the driveway, telling herself that first thing tomorrow she would clean out the garage so there would be enough space. She went inside and chilled, deciding to spend the rest of the evening just relaxing until Roy came over after meeting Hakim.

Lorna had no idea what she had just done by getting Marcus' car. With it now parked out in her driveway, the plates facing the street, her home would suddenly take on new meaning. The wind blew, causing the snow to drift over the sidewalks and the driveway around her house. The naked trees blew, icy chunks of snow gathering on their branches. Gloomy skies that sat over the city made the neighborhood look all the more eerie, as there seemed to be very little going on around Lorna.

Chapter 3

Kayla felt as if for once in the last few days she had actually been blessed with God's grace. She felt so lucky that she and her family were able to go back to their home and get things they needed. Latrell and Linell stuck to the plan, going upstairs to their bedrooms and getting enough clothes to last for the week – five outfits. When Kayla went back to her room, having to look in her closets to see if there were any visitors, was something that she had never thought she would have to do. Every second seemed to be two seconds for everyone. Nerves were on edge at the very thought of the two crazy dudes with guns coming back. They had really done a number on Rolanda and her children, making this something that they'd never forget.

Once they were out of the house and on their way back to Lyesha's house, their nerves were able to chill out a little bit. Kayla watched to be sure that there wasn't a car following them. Eventually, she gave in and admitted that she was probably being a little paranoid. If those fools came back again, it was probably right after going to the hospital. What are the real chances they would just so happen to be parked outside of their house when they go inside for ten minutes to gather up some things? Kayla thought about how unlikely that would be as she drove back over to Keystone, but she still felt frightened for her safety. The way the guy holding the gun over her mother had talked to her just imprinted into her mind.

When they got home, Kayla, who had grabbed some of her nicer clothes, spent the next hour or so getting ready. She was going to go to the library downtown and put in some job applications on the computer. Since Lyesha was at work, she wasn't able to get the code to the Wi-Fi account so that she could connect her computer to it. She'd brought some of her nicer clothes in case she had a job interview. Being prepared was the biggest goal for her, because she needed the money now more than ever.

Kayla slipped out of the house when her mother had gone upstairs to use the bathroom. Out in the snow, driving downtown, the streets suddenly felt unsafe. They hadn't felt that way before these dudes were after Marcus and coming to her family. To say the least, Kayla was uncomfortable. Any black car rolling by made her look twice, especially if the car had tinted windows. There were at least two or three instances where Kayla had thought she'd seen the car.

Down at the library, Kayla could see that things really hadn't changed a lot over the years. She found a spot to park right on the side of the library, on Pennsylvania Street. Inside, the reaction from the various men around the library was much the same as it had been when she was younger. After all, it had been some years since she'd been to the library. And Kayla quickly saw that a lot of things still hadn't changed. There were still a lot of bums in the library, as they'd spend their daytime hours there until the library closed and put them back out onto the street.

The six floors of the library were kind of busy. Kayla even walked by a couple of people she remembered from high school. She really didn't know either of them all that well, but did remember having some classes with them. From the looks of how they were dressed and who they were walking with, the two of them had gone on in life to do better for themselves. This inference – or assumption, if you will – put a little pep in Kayla's step. It also made her look more critically at what was going on in her life. Being on the run because of something her boyfriend got mixed up in was not really what she had planned for herself.

Kayla settled into a computer on the sixth floor. For the next couple of hours, she would apply for no less than ten jobs. She tried hotels, fast food restaurants, and even an insurance company that had a job posted that all an applicant needed was a high school diploma. She applied for a school janitor position, praying to God that this job wouldn't be the only one to call her back as they seemed to have the most desperate wording in their job advertisement. All of these positions did not do much for

Kayla's self-esteem, but she kept on pushing, knowing that she needed the money. Her mother didn't even look as if she was going to try to do a damn thing to pull her family up the least bit. And Kayla found that to be so sad.

When Kayla had just finishing applying at a hotel out by the airport, a guy sat down at the computer next to her. She was still answering a few questions about her job history that the hotel wanted to know. She noticed the guy at her side was looking over her way. In fact, there were moments when Kayla felt as if he were almost staring at her. Kayla turned and smiled, noticing that he was a black guy and was kind of intelligent looking. He wore glasses and had this very studious look about him. At his side, on the floor, set one of those brown bags that Kayla saw people downtown carrying.

The man smiled back as he logged onto the computer. He then glanced at Kayla's computer screen.

"I know how you feelin'," this guy said.

Kayla, judging by his voice, figured this dude to be around thirty-five or thirty-six years old. He was handsome, and unlike any kind of guy she had ever talked to. She noticed how he was looking in her eyes, then down at her shapely body as her backside filled the library chair. A portion of her ass spilled out of the back of the seat, catching the man's attention.

"Yeah," Kayla said. She smiled and looked back at her computer screen to finish putting in information so she could get out of there. The library was such a nice building, but it was swarming with bums. She was just happy that a normal person had sat down next to her for once. "This shit is tiresome, I swear it is. But I gotta find me something and I gotta find it soon."

The man had logged into his computer and appeared to be pulling out some documents.

"What kind of work are you looking for?" he asked.

Kayla could immediately see that this guy was educated, judging by the way he spoke.

Kayla shrugged. "I don't know," she answered. "I'm just lookin' for anything that will give me some hours at this point. I'm not real picky. Just need some money and need it for a while."

The guy snickered, nodding his head. "You're really trying to get out there and get that money, huh?" he asked, coming across very nice. "Well, what do you think about working at this call center?"

"Call center?" Kayla asked. She'd never even thought about trying to get a job at a call center. "What kinda call center?"

The guy looked Kayla up and down again. "It's nothing hard," he said. "You just call people on behalf of the library and update them on their accounts with us, such as what books they have open and stuff. I could get you on."

"The library?" Kayla asked, turning away from her screen. "You work here?"

The dude nodded. "Yeah," he answered. "I work down on the first floor. When you come in, remember seeing offices? I work back there. I can get you on if you want."

Kayla nodded as she thought about it. Part of her wanted to ask how much this job paid, but she didn't want to push her luck and come across as tacky. She looked the guy up and down, wondering why he would just come out and actually offer her a job. He didn't even know her. However, at this point, she just didn't have the time to find out. If she could get a job – any job – because of this man, she was going to give it a go and go with the program.

"Yeah," Kayla said, shrugging and smiling. "I mean, that's sounds like it'd be a nice job. How do I apply?"

Just then, the guy looked at his phone. "We can go downstairs now and I can get you in touch with the human resources lady," he said. "She'd be able to tell you how to apply the best because I don't know if it's through the website."

Kayla felt like maybe – just maybe – God was finally shining a little light on her. What are the chances that she would meet a guy who would see her for what she really was and help her get ahead a little? She still kept her guard up, but was open to there being positive people in the world.

The two of them introduced themselves to the other before getting up and heading toward the escalator. On the way down, as they talked, Kayla noticed how this guy, whose name was Jonathon, always managed to wind up walking behind her in some way. She could really sense that he was admiring her body. The attention was nice, had it been in passing. However, as they headed downstairs, it did make the walk seem a little longer.

Once they got down to the first floor of the library, Kayla wasn't so nervous. She had gotten into quite a conversation with Jonathon. He was really showing her his best side – coming across as just a genuinely good dude. Kayla waited outside of the glass office doors that appeared to be leading back into a maze of offices. A few minutes later, Jonathon came walking down the hall with a tall, older white woman. Kayla put on her best personality when she talked to the white woman, watching how well she spoke and her mannerisms. She smiled and remained perky the entire time.

The human resources lady went ahead and took Kayla's information. Because she had something else to do, she couldn't interview her right now or else she would. However, all of this happening did give Kayla some optimism. Once she had finished talking to the library's human resources person, Jonathon walked at her side as she headed toward the back doors of the library.

"Thank you so much," Kayla said, smiling. "She seemed really nice."

"She is," Jonathon said. "I can tell when she likes someone, and it definitely looks to me like she likes you. Just, when you do get the interview, show her how pretty of a person you are." Jonathon's eyes feasted on Kayla. "And you just might be working here. They really need somebody to get on that phone."

"Well," Kayla said. "I can definitely do that. I hope she does call me."

"Speaking of calling you," Jonathon said. "I should get your number so I can let you know what I hear or anything about other jobs around here."

Kayla hesitated for a moment. She then realized that if she wanted to get out in the world and do for herself, she would need to be a little easy going when it came to meeting dudes. This dude had just gotten her hooked up with a possible job. While she did feel him looking at her body, the fact of the matter is that he didn't take it a step further. Kayla went ahead and traded numbers with him, the two of them saving the other's number into their phone.

Kayla gave Jonathon a quick hug before pushing the library doors open. She walked in the cold wind that whipped between the apartment buildings on the north end of downtown. When she passed a courtyard of one building, the wind collided with the building and bounced off, causing snow to blow back into her face, particularly her eyelashes. By the time she got back to the car and got inside, she was practically shaking to get the snow off of her. Before she pulled out, she checked her text messages as usual. There was a text message from Jonathon. It read:

It was really nice meeting you today, Kayla. Like I said, it really does seem like the director likes you. I know I saw something in you that would be good for that job.

Kayla smiled, liking the compliment. She sent a reply, thanking Jonathon. Within a matter of seconds, another text message popped up from Jonathon.

No problem. Maybe we could get together sometime and talk about other ways you could get a little money going. Let me know when you're free and maybe we can chill.

Right away, Kayla's mind went to the obvious question: What did Jonathon mean by *other ways you could get a little money going*? Kayla thought about how he looked her up and down, doing very little to hide just how attracted he was to her. Kayla realized what he was doing, and she hated herself for falling for it. As she drove, curse words slipped out of her mouth as it all became clearer to her now that the man who could have just gotten her on at the library, doing a job that would be far better than slinging burgers at McDonald's or Burger King, really had one thing on his mind.

***

Later on, when Kayla got home, she felt her mother's eyes scold her as she walked through the front door.

"And where the hell you been?" Rolanda asked, looking at her daughter. "I was thinkin' about callin' you, but I wasn't sure if you would answer."

Kayla rolled her eyes as she slid out of her coat and placed it on the back of a chair in the dining room. Rolanda, apparently, had just gotten back herself. On the dining room table set a bag of Chinese carryout food – what Kayla guessed to be dinner.

"I was out lookin' for a job," Kayla answered. "And I think I mighta found one."

Rolanda's entire disposition changed. While she could have her moments at times, she did like the idea of her daughter getting a job. Whatever Kayla brought in would make her burden a lot less, or at least that's how Rolanda saw it. She encouraged Kayla to continue.

Kayla filled her mother in on how she'd applied for numerous jobs on the computer. She met a man who worked at the library – a man who had told her about a job opening. Once Kayla finished up talking about how the guy had taken her down to the library's first floor to talk to the human resources lady, Rolanda shook her head.

"Hmm, hmm," Rolanda said. "You know what that nigga is really after. Don't think cause he was professional or something that he ain't out here try'na get the same thing as these other niggas and shit. Them professional types, Kayla, can be the freakiest of them all."

Thoughts of what Jonathon said in the text message scrolled across Kayla's mind. The more and more she thought about it, the more and more she was coming to the conclusion that he was low-key propositioning her to sell him some pussy. She was offended – or at least, would be – if that was the case. However, she began to look at how her getting the job and or keeping it could be affected by what this man wanted out of her. Beyond that, she had to stop and think for a second about why the idea didn't completely turn her off.

Thirty minutes later, Latrell and Linell were sitting across from Rolanda and Kayla as Kayla ate a box of shrimp fried rice. Just then, Lyesha walked through the door, coming home from work.

"Hey, girl," Rolanda greeted her best friend. "We got some for you, too."

Lyesha let out a deep breath as she walked through the kitchen and into the dining room. After setting her bag on the steps, she sat down. Her beauty, especially well-done with makeup, could not be overlooked. So many throughout the years, would compare her to Rasheeda from *Love and Hip Hop Atlanta*. However, there were differences; Lyesha was a bit shorter and had a different texture of hair.

After dinner, the house quickly died down. Rolanda made Latrell and Linell go to bed at their normal bedtime. It had been decided that Rolanda would get up in the morning and take them to school. Kayla appreciated the gesture, but she seriously doubted it would actually happen. While she nodded at her mother making a commitment, she went ahead and prepared herself mentally to get up the next morning to take Latrell and Linell to school. It is what it is, or at least that was how Kayla saw it.

When the living room got dark, Kayla eventually could hear her mother snoring. She looked past her mother, thanks to the light of the television making it possible for her to see at all, and could see that Linell and Latrell were knocked out cold. Kayla took this as her opportunity to get up and head down to the basement. She opened the basement door and softly stepped down, on the tips of her toes, until she got down to the back corner, by the washer and dryer. Kayla liked how Lyesha's basement was actually finished and looked as if she'd done some updating. Kayla leaned against the washer and called Marcus. She had never felt so relieved to hear his voice.

"Wassup?" Marcus answered. He clearly sounded happy to hear Kayla's voice.

Kayla could not help but smile. "Hey," she said. "How is it up there?"

Marcus groaned. "It's cool," he said. "I'm already ready to get back down to Nap, though. I don't like this sitting around stuff. I swear I don't. And being at my cousin's apartment and I don't really even know him like that."

"What kinda neighborhood is he in?" Kayla wanted to know.

"Nothin' special, but nothin' bad," Marcus told her. "It's kinda suburban and shit. Retention ponds with geese and shit."

Kayla giggled at the way Marcus talked about the retention pond. "Oh, okay," she said.

"I talked to my uncle," Marcus said.

"What he say?" Kayla asked, now starting to feel more concerned. "Did he hear anything?"

"He ain't say that he heard anything," Marcus explained. "But he did tell me that he was already in the works with try'na get in touch with Hakim."

"In touch with Hakim?" Kayla asked. "What's he going to do with that? Do Hakim even know, already, that your uncle is your uncle? That sound like it could be a bad setup, Marcus."

"Damn," Marcus said, listening to what Kayla was telling him. She had a point. "You right. I mean, I'm sure my uncle would have thought of that before he reached out to the nigga and was try'na make plans to go over there. He ain't no dummy or nothin'."

"You right," Kayla said. "Your uncle is going to do something about this. I'm just kinda scared about what he's going to do."

"Me too," Marcus said. "I told him to not kill nobody, but then again, I don't know if I was sayin' that shit because I want to kill the nigga myself once my arm get back to workin' and shit. I got all this fuckin' frustration buildin' up in me that I almost can't take this shit...just sittin' here and can't do nothin'. All I'm doin' right now is thinkin' about how I wanna kill that nigga myself for all this shit he doin'."

"Marcus, don't say no shit like that," Kayla said. She glanced up the basement steps, glad that the house was quiet. She remembered to speak softly so she wouldn't wake anyone up, turning herself toward the wall in the corner. "And I don't know what your uncle gon' do, but he prolly gon' come through and fix all of this for you. He been there for you since forever, so we both know that he ain't gon' do nothin' that would make your situation even worse."

"Yeah," Marcus said. "You right. I was just lettin' you know, though. He also said that I can't tell my mama that I was talkin' to his ass." Marcus chuckled. "Basically, he said that my mama told him that she blame him for gettin' me involved in this lifestyle and shit like that. So, because of this shit happening, she wants me to not talk to him no more. She also want me to watch what I say to my boys Brandon and Juan. You know how my mama is."

"Yeah," Kayla said, reflecting back to when she was sitting right next to Miss Lorna. "Your mama sure do not like them two, I can tell you that."

"I know she don't," Marcus said. "I know. But I been textin' them too, but I ain't told them where I am. I really don't think they had anything to do with this, but just in case they did, which I really, really don't think, it would be betta if they ain't know where I was at or nothin' like that. They went and got them some heat."

"Some heat?" Kayla asked, sounding surprised. "You mean them niggas went and got themselves some guns?"

Kayla listened to Marcus rattle off the names of the guns. "Awe, naw," Kayla said. "What the fuck y'all try'na do?"

"What you mean what we try'na do?" Marcus asked, his tone sounding very defensive. "I'mma do whatever I can to get these niggas before they get you or my ass. I'm more concerned about you, if you must know."

"Marcus, don't worry about me," Kayla said. "We doing okay at the moment. We went back and got some stuff from the house and everything was fine. We back at my God…" Kayla caught herself. "We back at my mama's friend's house over by the White Castles. We be all right, for a minute anyway."

"Yeah, but still," Marcus said. It was very clear that he had had some time on his hands – time that had been used for him to think. "Fuck that nigga," he said. "It look like we probably are gon' have to kill his ass. Look at what the fuck he did, for some shit that I ain't even do. He shot up my shit, like we in Compton or somewhere. Then, his fuckin' niggas came into your house and held you family hostage like some fuckin' terror shit or somethin'. What you think we gon' have to do? Call the police so they can investigate? You already know them white people ain't gon' do shit but simply arrest everybody involved and convict. Ain't no point in even going that route."

Kayla nodded, listening to Marcus. He had several good points. The system was not going to work in anyone's favor in this situation.

"You just make sure you be watchin' your shit, you know?" Marcus said. "And I'mma get back down there as soon as I can, I promise you that. I ain't gon' be sittin' up here for long."

"Marcus, you know your mama want you to stay up there and wait this shit out," Kayla reminded him. "Why you gon' make this even harder for her by you coming back down here?"

"It ain't gon' be harder for her," Marcus said. "She ain't gon even know that I'm comin' back down there."

"You gon' fuckin' come down here and hide?" Kayla asked, surprised at all of the covertness. "What is this? Some Diary of Anne Frank bullshit or something? What are we, the Jews or something? How you gon' get back down here in the first place, Marcus? You know your cousin prolly ain't gon be the one to go for helpin' you get back down here."

"I know, I know," Marcus said. "I ain't figured all that out yet. With me not tellin' Brandon and Juan that a nigga is up in Fort Wayne, that limits my options a lot more. I'mma figure all that out, though. And it's gon' be a minute before I really decide when."

Kayla and Marcus continued on with their conversation for a few more minutes. It came to a point where Kayla realized that she had better head back upstairs. She needed to go to sleep, on the couch in Lyesha's living room, so that she could be ready to be up in the morning for Latrell and Linell. When she said bye to Marcus, it was truly somewhat of a sad moment. It had gotten to the point where their communication was sporadic, which was a drastic change from how the two would text back and forth to one another practically non-stop just a couple of days ago.

When Kayla headed back upstairs, she made her way through Lyesha's dining room and back to her couch in the living room. The house was so quiet, the kind of quiet where you start to wonder if you are really hearing that ringing sound. Her mother must have woken up to turn the television off. All Kayla could do was think as she took the time to get comfortable. Eventually, her eyes were looking up toward the ceiling.

As Kayla's eyes adjusted to the darkness, she picked her phone up off of the floor. She read over Jonathon's text message from earlier. She thought about how she and Marcus really were there for one another, in hard times such as these. To say the least, Kayla struggled with becoming comfortable with the idea of keeping secrets from him. She didn't like that she was choosing to not tell him where she and her family were staying. Having to catch herself during the conversation was hard. Beyond that, there was the issue that was fresh on her mind: Jonathon and possibly getting the job at the library. For whatever reason, Kayla really thought about seeing what Jonathon was talking about. *Was he the kind of man to come up off of some money to spend a little time with a woman? If I say no to him, could I wind up not getting that job? God, I just don't wanna wind up working at a damn McDonalds or something. That just ain't me, I swear it ain't.*

Drowning in her own thoughts, Kayla felt a little pressure. She placed her phone back on the floor and went back to staring into the dark. She knew that she would have to make some sort of decision in the morning. The idea of stepping out on Marcus did not sit well with her. But then she remembered where she was sleeping tonight, and how she wound up there – a situation that did not sit well with her, either.

Chapter 4

When Roy pulled up outside of Hakim's home on Cold Springs Road, he could not help but to think, *Damn*. As if the neighborhood itself wasn't nice enough, Hakim had really kept this particular place in great condition. Roy had no doubt in his mind that Hakim had multiple homes around Indianapolis, and probably some in small towns outside of the city. There was no way he'd just have one address.

Roy sized up the property as he slowed to turn into the driveway. Surrounded by a wrought-iron gate at the front was a white brick, ranch-styled house. The driveway curved in, through a wooded front yard, and curved around a little statue up by the garage doors. There seemed to be a hill at the back of the house, leading down into even more wooded areas. The houses in every direction were top notch as well. Hakim clearly had some gardening work done on the property; with some of the flowers Roy saw, he would have been inclined to think that white people lived in this house. It went so well with everything else, and this sure wasn't the kind of neighborhood where someone would be likely to find too many blacks.

Once Roy rung the buzzer, he felt under his car seat for his gun and slid it into his inside pocket. He'd made sure to bring it with him when he left the house, never knowing what exactly could break out. Just in case he needed a little protection, he thought it'd be better to bring it. As his mother used to always tell him when he was a child: it's better to need it and to have it then to need it and to not have it. Truer words had never been spoken, especially for a time like this.

Hakim unlocked the driveway gates from inside the house. They slowly swung open and Roy rolled forward. The trees in the front yard hugged the road as they towered over Hakim's house by what looked like several stories. The neighborhood was so quiet that all Roy could hear were his tires rolling against the pavement and the cold wind blowing through bare branches.

Roy parked in front of the house. He saw there were no other cars in the driveway. This forced him to take note of the three-car garage and think about how many, and whose, cars could be in there. With caution, he stepped up to the door. The sound of a vicious Pit Bull came out of the basement windows.

Inside, Hakim welcomed Roy into his home. The two made eye contact immediately. Each other saw something in the other's eyes that made them keep their guard up. When Hakim shook Roy's hand, they hugged briefly before going into the family room. Roy took in Hakim's house, noticing how every piece of furniture in it was top notch, all the way down to the register grates and the light switch designs. As soon as they stepped into the dining room, Roy's eyes were pulled to a woman. She walked around, from the kitchen to the dining room, as if she was cleaning up. Her very plump ass was barely covered by short, black booty shorts. The way her ass cheeks hung out of the bottom of her shorts drove Roy crazy inside. However, it didn't take him long to remember how Marcus had gotten mixed up the wrong way with this guy. He immediately pulled his eyes off of the woman and put them back on Hakim.

Hakim, noticing how Roy looked a little too hard, got Amber's attention. She was cleaning up from where she'd cooked for Roy, Jayrone, and Raul. The food was good, and he was really grateful for that, telling her, "Baby, why don't you just go chill out for a second, huh? Clean that shit up later."

Amber, who was wearing a white t-shit that showed the impressions of her nipples, turned to Hakim. She walked over to him, and Roy watched the two of them kiss, with Hakim's hand rolling down to the small of her back before slapping her ass hard. She then walked away, disappearing as she headed toward what appeared to be the hallway for the bedrooms.

Hakim turned back to Roy. "You'll have to excuse me," he said, loving that he had a fine bitch to show off to a dude he had not seen in many years. "She gets a little worked up from time to time and I gotta calm her down, you know?"

"Yeah," Roy said, noticing how Hakim regarded women more as property than as human beings. "I feel you on that."

"So, have a seat my nigga," Hakim said, trying to sound hospitable.

While Hakim walked into the living room and came back, Roy looked him up and down. He still looked pretty fit after all of these years. Bulky, with big shoulders. It looked like he clearly worked out. Then again, there was no doubt about that at this point for Roy. He could look around Hakim's house and see how everything was dripping with money. Sure, he'd made some money in his lifetime, but nothing to the likes of Hakim.

"What's been up?" Hakim asked. "Ain't seen you since we used to see each other at them parties and shit, way back in the day."

"Yeah, man," Roy said, having a seat on a large, white sectional. He looked around, noticing how the ceiling in this room was higher than the rest, seeming to reach up into where there would be a form of attic space. The fireplace was bulky and commanding, built with painted white brick. Roy finally noticed that there was a balcony looking down above them, spanning about ten feet of the room's width. That, alone, made him a little nervous. "You know how life is. Shit gets busy."

Yeah, you been busy alright, Hakim thought as he walked back to the room with his bag of weed and some wraps. "You still smoke or what?" he asked.

"Yeah, man," Roy said. "I do."

"Cool," Hakim said. "I'mma roll this blunt up and we can talk. You man, I ain't even know that you was still involved in this shit. Hadn't heard about you or seen you in some years."

"Yeah," Roy said. "Not really out like I used to be. I mean, I'm still doin' this and that. That ain't never gon change.

I came up in this, but just do things a little different now. Don't be out so much as I used to be, back when I was younger."

"That's wassup, though," Hakim said, wondering about Roy's true intentions for reaching out to him. He went on with rolling the blunt. Soon enough, he handed the lighter and the blunt to Roy. "Hit that shit first, my nigga."

Cautiously, Roy took the blunt and lighter from Hakim. In the back of his mind, he couldn't help but wonder if maybe whatever he was smoking could be laced with something. He took one hit and really analyzed it, despite the lack of good that would do. Once he saw that it was just some good weed, he was able to relax a little bit. Still, however, his ears and eyes were on the lookout. This house appeared a lot larger inside than it did from the outside. Roy, out of the corners of his eyes, made sure to stay alert with the doors. He felt comfortable knowing that he had grabbed his gun and slid it into his inside coat pocket.

Hakim looked at Roy, knowing that something was up. He didn't even have to ask this dude Roy if he was Marcus' uncle. With what he knew now, and with how this dude was coming across, there was more to his reasoning for coming over here than *just* business. This felt very personal, almost as if Roy was going to come out and ask him about something that was very dear and close to him.

The conversation went here and there as the two caught up about old characters that they both knew from back in the day. Eventually, things got around to business.

"So, you hit me up because of some business shit?" Hakim asked, directly.

Roy nodded. "Yeah," he said. He quickly remembered all of the major points he had made in his head on the ride over. Whatever he said to Hakim had to come across genuine until he had the chance to really drop in some stuff that would give Roy the clues he needed to know if now would be the time to smoke him or not. Roy was very on edge about the fact that the house was so quiet and there were several rooms, not to mention two floors with a balcony, for a man who didn't appear to have a wife and children living with him. On top of that, there was just something about Hakim's demeanor. He really seemed like what could only be described as a hard ass nigga.

"Yeah, man," Roy said. "I heard about how you still out here, still makin' big moves and shit. That's why I thought to hit you up, and just so happen to hear your name again when I was meetin' up with George about some property."

"Yeah, he told me about that," Hakim said. "George... He a good dude. Ain't never tried to fuck me over, and the nigga ain't connected to nobody that has either."

Roy picked up on Hakim's tone with the word *connected*. He kept his eyes on Hakim while listening to any sound going on in or around the house. The wind blowing outside practically sounded like a train coming to him at this point.

"Yeah, he is a cool dude," Roy said. "But, yeah, so I'm ready to expand a little bit, bruh."

Hakim nodded. "Is that so?" he asked, thinking about the slim chance that this dude was truly just over here to talk business. He leaned in to listen. "Wassup?"

"I heard you the dude to go to if a nigga wanna get his shit from outta town," Roy said. "If a nigga wanna get more for his money so he can get it out in these streets and really make that money off of it."

"Yeah," Hakim said, nodding. "That would be me. I ain't get this far," he motioned toward the nice things he had around the house, "without being good at what I do. I always get what I go after."

Nodding, Roy said, "That's wassup, that's wassup." He then passed the blunt to Hakim.

"What would be a good way to work with a nigga so I can get connected down south and shit?" Roy asked.

"Well, let a nigga ask you this," Hakim said. "What city you try'na get your stuff out of?"

Just then, Roy took the plunge, not knowing how Hakim would react to his answer. "Texas," he said. "I know they got the shit in Dallas."

Hakim nodded his head, truly at a loss for words. If there was ever any doubt that this dude was Marcus' uncle, it had just been removed by his answer to that question. *What were the chances that he would say the very same place where Marcus went? What a big coincidence.* Hakim thought to himself.

"Yeah," Hakim said. "Dallas got that shit. But, I do gotta warn niggas, if you fuck with my shit in Dallas, then me and you got a problem."

"Oh yeah?" Roy asked. "Who would fuck with you to the point where they got a problem with you?"

Hakim chuckled. "I wonder the same thing myself," he said to Roy. "These niggas out here know how I am and shit. And you know what? Yet and still, I get niggas who try me. I get niggas who try to fuck a nigga over and shit and think that he ain't gon know. Even with what people know about me out in the hoods, I still get niggas who step to me about one thing when they really thinking about something else. Them be the kind of niggas that I have a problem with. Them be the kinda niggas I don't get along with."

"That's wassup," Roy said. Now, he was definitely feeling the tension that was coming off of Hakim. "Well, you ain't gotta worry about that with me," he said. Hakim then thought, *Cause I'mma just kill your ass so you ain't gotta worry about that kinda shit no more.*

"And I also got another thing that really gets niggas on my bad list," Hakim said.

"Oh yeah?" Roy said, wanting to hear. "What's that?" Roy could feel that Hakim knew something.

"My women," Hakim said. "I'm sure you already know how to conduct yourself and shit. We ain't gotta worry about that, now do we?"

"I heard about the nigga you put in the canal back when," Roy said. "Was that a nigga that fucked with your chick and shit?"

Hakim shrugged. "I don't remember, man," he said, very casually. "I don't even know which one you talkin' bout."

Roy looked back at the bedroom hallway, hearing what sounded like it could have been the chick moving. He still felt uneasy, knowing that Hakim would have something in the works for this meeting. Judging by some of the things he was saying, he was trying to imply what he was going to do with

Marcus while never actually bringing him up. When Hakim said he didn't know which one, the image of Marcus' body floating in the canal flashed in his mind. It took every piece of strength in his body to keep from jumping up and putting a bullet into Hakim's head. If he had his way, and had some backup with him or was on his own terms and in his own place, Hakim would have been laying out on the floor by this point. Roy would be more concerned with figuring out what he was going to do with his body than if he was going to be ambushed.

"Look nigga," Hakim said, now sounding very serious. "Why don't we stop all this fuckin' around and come right to the real reason you here? Nigga, I know you not here to talk about no business shit. Shit, we been in these streets for this long and you ain't never reached out to a nigga. Why the fuck you think I'mma just go for it now? I know why you here, my nigga."

Roy nodded, realizing that he had come to the point of no return. "Yeah?" he said. "You know why I'm here, huh?"

Hakim looked at him, setting the blunt in the ashtray on the glass coffee table that was between the two of them. "Nigga," he said to Roy. "You wouldn't happen to be any relation to this one dude I might be lookin' for, would you? A young nigga who fucked up and shit."

Roy nodded, wondering how Hakim knew that he was related to Marcus. "Depends," Roy said. "What you lookin' for him for and I might let you know if I'm related to the nigga or not?"

Hakim shook his head and smiled. "Nigga, where is he?" he asked, in a serious tone. "Don't know why y'all think you can hide the nigga forever. I'mma find his ass eventually, no matter what the little nigga think he gon' do. Ain't no rock I can't look under to find his ass and blow that damn head off."

Roy stood up. He could feel himself getting angry, not being able to take lightly how Hakim made threats on his family straight to his face. "Nigga, fuck you!" he said, his heart now racing as he figured his words would bring out whoever else might be hiding in the house. "Why the fuck you try'na kill a nigga for nothing?" he asked Hakim. "You really try'na kill him over some shit you say he took that we know he ain't take and some two-piece bitch?"

Hakim stood up. One of the very last things he ever allowed in his house was for another man to come in and disrespect him. Where he came from, that was enough grounds to wind up dead and found in a wooded area. However, as he had gotten older, he found these tactics to be a little too heinous to use at first. Instead, he chose to be a little more diplomatic with his approach. As long as the uncle was alive, he at least had a way of finding the nigga Marcus. Hakim knew that if he were to kill this dude right here and right now, he and his boys would be back at square one when it came to actually finding Marcus.

"Look, nigga," Hakim said to Roy. "I know you all in your feelings and shit over your nephew. I get it, and I understand." He paused. "But you gotta know too that I wasn't asking you if I was goin' to get his ass, I was telling you that I am going to get him. Ain't no doubt about it. Sooner or later, the little nigga gotta come up again."

"Nigga, fuck with my nephew and you really gon' have some problems," Roy warned.

Hakim chuckled. "Nigga, what kinda problem you think you can cause for me that I can't handle?" he asked him. "I don't guess you know how deep my hands go in these streets out here. For all you know," his voice lowered as he finished the sentence, "one of your neighbors could be workin' for me. George could be workin' for me, nigga."

Roy thought about the different influences, for lack of a better word, that Hakim had in the streets. He was a lot more aggressive in the game than Roy had been. Hakim was also better interconnected socially, whereas Roy was kind of pulled back and in the shadows of what was going on. Roy could not think of much to say. Rather, he'd thought about how he wanted to kill this nigga so bad. He could almost taste the blood from how much he wanted to jump on him.

"Where is he?" Hakim asked. "Look, Roy, you know the shit is only gonna get worse for him and everyone involved unless you just hand 'em over. Me and my boys ain't forgot about the little girlfriend, Kayla. We can't wait to get our hands on that fat ass I hear she got. That bitch gon' make good collateral, really get Marcus to show his face and stop runnin' scared like a little bitch. All he had to do was go down to Texas and bring my shit back so he could get the money. I come back, some of the shit is missin' and he done fucked my bitch. I'm like damn, dude must'a had a fuckin' death wish or something. Or maybe the nigga is just that fuckin' stupid."

Roy took a deep breath, hating that Marcus had even made the choice to step outside of his family and work with this ruthless motherfucker. Even by looking in his eyes, Roy could see that Hakim was the kind of dude who would not stop – the type of man who enjoyed the chase and the feeling of accomplishment that came with him finally getting his target and using that target to make a statement to anybody else. Roy saw very little coincidence in the fact that those targets wound up in public places that got everyone talking.

"Maybe you need to check with the bitch," Roy suggested. "Man, you and me been in this shit for a long time. You know how women make shit up and use the next nigga to make a nigga jealous. Let's not act like we back in high school and shit. I know you thought 'bout what if she took the work, the half a brick or whatever and said Marcus took it."

Hakim gave a few seconds of thought to what Roy was saying. "Okay, okay," he said. "But that still don't explain why my neighbor got a front row seat and watched Marcus's ass go up and down while he was smashin' Tweety on the fuckin' back porch. Next thing I know, a nigga get back from outta town and half his block know that some otha nigga done been over and been smashin' his chick. I got a reputation to uphold over there, and ya little nephew Marcus done dipped his dick in the wrong pussy."

Roy shook his head, turning away and walking toward the front door – the door that he'd used to enter the house. "Nigga, you ain't gotta take it this far," Roy said, feeling that any moment a couple of armed niggas were going to appear out of the many closed doors. "You ain't gotta take the shit this far, man."

"Nigga, fuck you and fuck that little nigga!" Hakim said, walking into the living room. "Just know that, whether ya fake ass like the shit or not, I'mma get the little dick and I'mma chop his damn dick off for fuckin' my chick for all my fuckin' neighbors to see and shit, and takin' my shit too. Fuck him. He gon' make good practice. Tell him I'll be seein' his ass real soon, one way or another."

It took Roy every bit of strength he had as a man to refrain from pulling his gun out and putting a bullet in Hakim's head right then and there. However, as he walked out into the snowy, wooded front yard and back to his car in the driveway, he couldn't help but to have his eyes open. For whatever reason, he really felt like he was being watched. The entire few seconds it took him to leave the house and walk to his car, he looked around the yard. Roy looked at which areas of the yard were more wooded; which areas had more bushes. He noticed where the basement windows were in relation to the hill at the back of the house. When he stepped onto the driveway pavement, he even took a few seconds to look toward the back of the house. It definitely looked as if the hill let down to a walkout basement. The land sloped up and down slightly until it collided with more wooded area. Roy noticed the way there was a small upstairs, toward the back of the house, which he thought was maybe the part that was above where he sat in the family room area.

Roy got into his car and turned the engine over. With every move he made, it sounded twice as loud. It was *that* quiet outside – not even the sound of a car slushing past on Cold Springs Road. Roy looked into the windows of Hakim's house as he backed down the driveway and waited for the gates to open. The entire time, one hand was on the steering wheel while another hand was on his gun, down to his side. Should any bullet start flying in his direction, he would be ready to fire back and really blow this shit up.

Once out on Cold Springs Road, Roy headed toward 38th Street. He called his sister to tell her that he was on his way to her house. During his entire drive to his sister's house, he did not notice a green minivan following him. For each block, and at every intersection, it had remained just far enough behind his car for him to never notice that it was there and following him.

When Roy pulled up outside of Lorna's house, he winced slightly. He'd been thinking about the look of loving to kill somebody that was in Hakim's eyes. He knew that everything Hakim said about getting Marcus were his true intentions. The last thing he wanted to see was Marcus' car parked in his sister's driveway. To make matters worse, the license plate of the car was facing the street. Roy parked and headed up to the door, not noticing that the green minivan was coming to a stop at the stop sign down the street. The driver noticed what house Roy was going into and turned the corner, slowly moving down the street. The minivan rolled by Lorna's driveway. Roy was now inside, but as luck would have it, the van slowed as it passed the driveway, Marcus' car, plain to see, parked in it. The driver smiled and continued on driving.

***

Hakim was leaning against the counter, enjoying some of Amber's silky mouth, when he heard his phone vibrating. His pants were bunched up down around his ankles. He instructed Amber to dig his cell phone out of his pocket and hand it to him. Once she did that, just as she was told, Hakim immediately pushed her head back down onto his manhood. The audacity of that nigga Roy fronting on some bullshit to come over to his house and try to save his little nephew had gotten him all worked up. If he had been younger, he would've killed that nigga right on the spot – right over there, in the family room.

Hakim answered his phone, seeing that it was Raul calling. "Wassup?" he answered. Hakim greatly anticipated hearing what they had found out. The plan was for them to be parked in the driveway of a vacant house down the block. Once they saw Roy come out of the driveway, they were to pull out into the road and follow him at a distance. Nobody would ever suspect a suburban-mom minivan, and that was the exact reason Hakim patted himself on the back for picking up the van at an auction. It'd proven to be one of his biggest, and most covert, asset.

"Wassup, Hakim? It's Raul." He coughed. "We followed the nigga like you said, and you won't guess what we found."

"What?" Hakim asked, wondering if stupidity ran in the family with Roy and Marcus. Why in the world would he ever come over here and think that Hakim wouldn't have somebody ready to follow his ass back to wherever he went?

"We don't know who house this is," Raul explained. "But it's over on the east side and shit. He parked out front and Marcus's car is parked here too, right up in the driveway."

"Right in the driveway?" Hakim asked. "Y'all gotta be fuckin' kiddin' me. Now I know these niggas got stupid runnin' through the family."

Raul laughed, telling Jayrone next to him what Hakim had said. Jayrone laughed, calling Marcus and his family *stupid niggas*.

"So," Raul said. "What you want for us to do, Hakim? You want us to sit over here and see if we see Marcus or what?"

Hakim thought about it for a minute, holding the phone back from him as he told Amber to continue with what she was doing. Gladly, Amber smiled, grabbing the base of Hakim's manhood as she went harder, giving her best.

"Let's do this," Hakim said, as he began to explain his plan.

***

Once inside of his sister's house, it was very clear that Roy was pissed off.

"What the fuck are you thinkin'?" Roy asked Lorna, who had just opened the door for him. The two of them walked back to the kitchen, where she had chicken in the oven and potatoes on the stove. "Are you fuckin' kiddin' me?"

"What, what?" Lorna asked, trying to figure out why her brother was so worked up. "What the fuck are you talkin' about, Roy?"

"You got Marcus's car over here?" Roy asked, shaking his head.

"Well, yeah," Lorna said. "I went and got it earlier. My friend took me over there to get it."

"That's all well and fine and shit, Lorna," Roy said. "But why you got it parked out in your driveway. Now, anybody riding by can see and maybe somebody riding by will know, or think, that it's Marcus's car. Damn. You even got the fuckin' license plate facing the street and shit, Lorna."

Lorna thought about it for a moment, realizing that Roy was right. "Damn," she said. "I wasn't thinking. I was so tired when I got back that I just parked it in the driveway. I ain't even think about how I would have to clean some space out of the garage."

"I'mma help you," Roy said. "The sooner, the better, too. So, just go on and finish up with your cookin' and stuff. I just went and saw Hakim."

Lorna's face became extremely serious. "Oh, you did?" she asked, looking Roy up and down. "And what did he say, Roy?"

Roy's hesitation was enough for Lorna to know that whatever Hakim had said wasn't good. Eventually, Lorna had to sit down at the kitchen table after turning the stove off. Hearing what all Hakim had said to Roy really made her realize that this nigga was going to try to kill her son.

Chapter 5

Lorna found it incredibly difficult to fall asleep that night. If this had been any other day, such as a day when she hadn't just taken her son two hours away to hide from a bullet, she would've fallen to sleep easily from all the activity. However, today was different. There were times she thought that she was nodding off to sleep, only to have her eyes pop wide open minutes later as if it were first thing in the morning.

Roy had left only a few hours ago, giving Lorna the dreaded account of what Hakim had said. There were moments where Lorna wondered why her brother told her. Beyond that, she was starting to not be so against Roy's plans on really going after Hakim before he got to Marcus.

Lorna slid out of bed. The hardwood floors underneath her bedroom carpet creaked terribly. Since there was no other noise in the house, all she could hear was her footsteps and the wind blowing past and around the house, making a howling noise. Lorna walked casually down her dark hallway and into the kitchen. Just as she put a kettle of water onto the stove, so she could make some tea, she heard what sounded like crunching sounds. Furthermore, they sounded as if they were coming from outside.

Quickly, the half-sleep Lorna woke up fully. She turned the kitchen light off, slowly turning around to see if she heard the crunching noises again. Once she hadn't heard any more for a few seconds, she stepped over to a window and looked out at her backyard. Just as she had parted the curtain, only a few inches, what would normally be the view of a wide open snow-covered backyard, was cut off by a man walking in front of her kitchen window.

Lorna's reaction was to quickly step back from the window. She looked out, from a few feet back, seeing what looked like the shadow of a man. First, he walked in front of one window, then another. Next thing she knew, he was stepping up to her back door. Quickly, Lorna turned around and ran back to her bedroom. She dug her gun out as she heard what sounded like somebody pushing the back door. At this point, her heart was racing. All she could think about was Kayla and her account of two armed men coming into their home and holding them all as hostages. Lorna told herself that something like that just wasn't going to happen to her. She was going to be ready to put up a fight. *Nobody knows your house better than you do*, Lorna thought to herself as she remembered hearing that on a true crimes episode about a serial killer in Wichita, Kansas.

Once Lorna's gun was loaded, she stepped out into her hallway. She could look down and see her living room, where little rays of light came in from between the curtains. She immediately pressed her back against a wall and moved slowly toward the front of the house. As soon as she had gotten a few feet into her journey, she heard the back door being kicked in. Without thinking, she dipped into one of her spare bedrooms. Never in her life had she been so frightened as she was then. Not only had her back door been kicked in but it also sounded as if there were two sets of footsteps making their way through the kitchen. Lorna could hear their wet, ice-chipped-covered shoes crunching against the linoleum floor. She cocked the gun and held it up, the barrel now pointed toward the ceiling as Lorna listened closely.

Raul and Jayrone, with Jayrone following behind, both held their guns. They hated when Hakim would have them go into strange houses. Sure, this house wasn't all that big, but it was darker than the rest. Clearly, whoever lived here preferred thick curtains to stop anyone from seeing inside. They'd checked a couple of windows with no luck before finding that some windows in the back were in the kitchen. This is when they decided to go in through the back door. It only helped them that this house was a little further apart from its neighbors, making it less likely that the next house down would hear the door being kicked in.

Raul stepped out into the living room, holding his gun tight. Out of the corner of his eyes, he looked down the hallway, as it practically disappeared into a dark pit. He then pulled a door open, figuring that it led down. Just as he'd thought, there were steps leading down to a basement. This alone would make his job all the harder to find whoever was in this house. No matter what they did, however, they remembered to step as lightly as they could.

Lorna tried her hardest to breathe quietly as she ducked inside of a closet in one of her spare bedrooms. It was so obvious to her that whoever was in her house was trying to walk as quietly as they could. At times, she could hear the ice on the bottoms of their shoes crunching. Other times, she almost couldn't hear anything. All she knew was that she was going to hold her gun firmly and be ready to pull the trigger at a moment's notice. They weren't going to get her and do her the way they'd done Kayla's family.

Raul motioned for Jayrone to check the basement. As he headed down the steps, Raul checked the front room and the dining room. These rooms were clear – nothing but darkness. Raul headed down the bedroom hallway, the area of the house that made him the most nervous. On both sides were doors. And he didn't know which doors were the bathroom and which were the bedrooms. Carefully, he stepped up to the first door and slightly put his head out. It was the bathroom, and it was empty. All he had to do was flip the light on quickly to see nothing but a sink, bathtub, and toilet. He turned the light off and moved on, moving down the hallway toward the second door, which was on his left now.

Raul peered into that room, seeing nothing. However, it did look as if it had been lived in. Stuff was a bit out of place, at least compared to the rest of the house. On top of that, it looked as if the bed had definitely been slept in. This obviously was not the master bedroom, seeing as it was missing a bathroom. From this, Raul could deduct that someone else had been staying in this house – the someone else probably being Marcus.

Raul moved on down the hallway, where he came to the master bedroom. With the way the hallway was configured, he was able to see into the bedroom before he actually came to the doorway. Once there, however, he cautiously looked inside. With the little bit of light that was coming from the street light out front into the bedroom, Raul could see that someone had obviously just gotten out of bed.

This caused his ears to perk up, as he was now realizing that he was definitely in the house with someone other than Jayrone. He smiled, the most crooked smile of all smiles, as he thought about how this was truly turning out to be a hunting game.

Raul held his gun toward the ceiling as he stepped further into the master bedroom. He checked under the bed, seeing nothing but shoes and bags. He then looked into the closet. It too was packed to the max, meaning that nobody would ever be able to hide in it, especially not on short notice. Raul then quietly stepped into the master bathroom. It was quite a nice size. After checking behind the shower curtain, he went back to the bedroom, then to the doorway of the hallway. There was only one room – that he was aware of – for him to check. This was the room across the hall from the master bedroom. Raul softly stepped out into the hallway and across.

Meanwhile, Jayrone was coming up with nothing down in the basement. In fact, it had looked as if nobody had even been down in the basement for some years. While it was finished, it was also very cluttered. On top of that, nothing really looked out of place. Jayrone headed back upstairs, his eyes meeting with the silhouette of Raul's body at the end of the bedroom. Raul flinched, looking down the hallway. He pointed into the remaining bedroom, letting Jayrone know that whoever was here was probably inside of this bedroom.

Quickly, Jayrone checked his surroundings and lightly stepped down the hallway. Raul went ahead and entered the bedroom. Instead of stepping all the way in, he knew that whoever was here would be better caught by surprise. Once he and Jayrone had both of their guns raised, Raul flipped the light switch. The bedroom lit up – immediately, Raul and Jayrone saw Lorna. A sheer look of terror was written all over her face when she saw that two guns in the hands of two men who were facing dead at her. She screamed.

"Bitch, shut up!" Raul told her. "Put the fuckin' gun down, bitch! Or we gon' blow your fuckin' head off."

Lorna, realizing that she was outnumbered, began to lower her gun to the floor. But more than anything, she wanted to shoot the both of them. Once she'd gotten halfway down to the floor, she quickly pulled her gun back up and fired. Lorna unloaded her gun, over and over, until all she could hear was clicking. She'd used her all of her bullets. When she opened her eyes, with her ears ringing, she was terrified to realize that the men had ducked out of the way. Within a matter of seconds, they were lunging toward her. She kicked and screamed, throwing her arms about. However, both men were just too strong for her, as well as too young. Lorna put up a good fight but wasn't able to stop them from holding her by her arms and lifting her up off of the floor. Lorna felt herself being thrown across the room and onto the bed. Once she turned over, she looked into the eyes of a couple of evil niggas with guns pointed at her. She crawled further up onto the bed.

"What the fuck y'all want with me?" Lorna asked, yelling. "Huh? What the fuck y'all want with me? Why y'all come here fuckin' with me?"

"Damn," Jayrone said, licking his lips. Seeing Lorna fall onto her stomach on the bed had given him a great view of her backside. She was a little up there in years, for his taste, but her body was still badder than a lot of chicks out here who would be young enough to be her daughter. On top of that, she had hips, which were practically bursting at the seams of her pink pajama pants. "This bitch got ass."

Raul nodded. "Hmm, hmm," he said, looking back at his boy. He then looked at Lorna, making sure to keep his gun on her. "Where is he?"

"Where is who?" Lorna said, feeling very uncomfortable with what the two men were saying about her. However, there was just no way in Hell that she was going to tell them where her son was. Marcus was her only child and she would do anything to protect him. "Who the fuck y'all talkin' about?" Lorna asked, trying to sound as clueless as possible.

"Now the bitch wanna sound dumb, don't she?" Raul asked, looking back at Jayrone and snickering. "Bitch, you know who the fuck we lookin' for," he said, nodding his head. "So, why don't you just tell us where he is so shit just goes real simple. We saw his car out in the driveway earlier, before you put it in the garage. Now, tell me where the fuck this nigga is! We got somebody that is lookin' for his ass."

"Fuck you," Lorna said. "And fuck whoever is fuckin' lookin' for my son. I ain't tellin' you where he is. I don't give a fuck what you do."

"Son?" Raul asked, his face saying that he found what he'd just heard to be very interesting. "Well, lookie here," he said. "This is the nigga's mama."

Jayrone licked his lips, as he'd always had a thing for thick, older women. And Lorna fit just about every qualification for him, with a little attitude to match. "Well, ain't that something," he said, looking at Raul. "This is the nigga's mother."

Raul nodded. "Hakim will be real interested to know that," he said. "Just wait till Marcus find out that we got his mama, and did shit to get her to tell."

"I don't give a fuck what y'all do to me!" Lorna yelled, feeling brave despite having guns pointed at her in her own home. "I ain't tellin' y'all where Marcus is."

Raul looked at Lorna and chuckled before moving toward the bed. "C'mon, nigga," he said to Jayrone, motioning toward Lorna. "Let's get this bitch outta here and over to Hakim's."

"Y'all not takin' me out in the cold with no clothes on!" Lorna yelled. "Y'all not gon' do that to me."

"Look here, bitch," Raul said. "I could let you put some clothes on, but I wouldn't want you workin' too hard, you probably ain't gonna need them much where we takin' you. So, just save your time and c'mon here so nobody has to get hurt…yet."

"No!" Lorna yelled. "No, no, no."

Just then, Raul moved in closer to Lorna. The barrel of the gun pointing at her caused her to freeze as Raul moved in closer and closer, rubbing her legs. "I smell you," he said. "And I can tell you got that good pussy, don't you?" Suddenly, Raul was backing away with the side of his face stinging. Lorna had slapped him with everything she had and moved further away from him.

Raul, rubbing the side of his face, backed away and stood up. He shook his head, almost wanting to laugh at this woman because she didn't know what she'd just done. He glanced at Jayrone, nodding his head because he already knew what was about to happen. When Raul looked back at Lorna, he began to undo his pants. "Bitch, I'm bout to show you what the fuck I'mma do to you," he said.

"Wait, man," Jayrone said. "What about Hakim? You already know this nigga gon' know if you fucked her first. Then, he gon' be lookin' for your ass the same way he got us lookin' for Marcus."

Raul nodded, looking at Lorna and seeing his buddy's point. "You right, you right," he said. "But if Hakim ain't try'na get in this pussy, I'm definitely gettin' in it. I don't let no bitch slap me. She just worked up and probably need some dick. C'mon, let's get her ass outta here and over to Hakim's."

Lorna resisted as the two men pointed guns at her and forced her down the hallway. Before she knew it, she was heading out into the snow. She looked out of the corners of her eyes at her block. So many of her neighbors' homes looked quiet. She prayed to God, as the men forced her down the walkway toward a green minivan parked out on the street, that one of her neighbors had heard the gunshots and called the police. The closer she got to the van, however, the less likely all of that seemed. The cold wind caused her to shake as the men rubbed her body, sometimes in inappropriate ways, until opening the van door. Lorna was pushed into the van. When she had turned around, the van door was already closing. The lit snowy outside had disappeared in a matter of second.

No sooner than she adjusted to being in the back of the van, Raul and Jayrone got into the front seats. Just as Raul was pulling off, Jayrone looked back at Lorna, with his gun pointing at her. "Try something bitch and you gon' wished you didn't," he said. "And I'm not gon' kill you. Naw..." His head shook. "I'mma make sure you stay alive until we through with you and you tell us where that nigga is." Jayrone then looked down at Lorna's thick thighs, looking attractive in her pajama pants. He stuck his tongue out of his mouth. "I'mma have a lot of fun with you."

Lorna backed away from the front seats toward the back of the van. After seeing that the van doors had some sort of child safety lock on them, she leaned in a corner. Raul and Jayrone were talking back and forth to one another for most of the ride, with Jayrone looking back at Lorna every so often and reminding her of the power he had in the gun.

They got onto the highway, which killed Lorna's idea of breaking one of the windows when they'd pull up to a stoplight. Rather, she felt cold as the van was moving at probably seventy miles an hour, around I-465 then down I-70. Soon enough, the highway was curving through the cluster of lit-up high rises that made up downtown Indianapolis. Lorna prayed to God that a police car would ride by, so she'd at least have the chance to get someone's attention who could do something about this.

Within twenty minutes or so, Raul was pulling the van up outside of Hakim's gate on Cold Springs Road. He called inside. When Hakim answered, it was clear that he'd been waiting for whatever would come back from Raul and Jayrone's assignment.

"Wassup?" he answered, as he pressed the buttons in the kitchen to open the gates.

"We got his mama," Raul said.

"And she a thick one too!" Jayrone said, loud enough for Hakim to hear through the phone.

Hakim simply told them to hurry up and get inside with her. Raul pulled the van up to the garage, opened one of the doors, and parked inside. As soon as the garage door closed – they waited because Hakim had the kinds of neighbors who actually attended their Neighborhood Watch meetings – Raul and Jayrone hopped out of the van. They swung the door open, grabbing the resistant Lorna by her arms. When she got out onto the garage pavement, Jayrone slapped her ass as if she was a stripper and told her to calm down.

Once inside, Lorna was pushed into a spare room in the basement that Hakim had used for the last few years as a fifth bedroom. It was a basic room outfitted with old furniture that Hakim had inherited when his grandparents died. Once Lorna bounced against the bed, turning over, she looked around and watched as the bedroom door closed.

"Where the fuck am I?" Lorna yelled. "Where the fuck am I? Where did y'all take me?"

Jayrone popped back into the door, pointing the gun at Lorna. "Bitch, would you shut the fuck up?" he said. "I'mma get in here as soon as I can and drop some dick in you. I know that's all you need."

Lorna looked at the man, shaking her head. "You are fuckin' disgustin," she said, the disgust apparent in her face.

Jayrone closed the door as Raul went to get Hakim.

"Nigga, this bitch is thick too," Raul said when he ran into Hakim upstairs. "In all the right places."

"Y'all ain't fuck her, did you?" Hakim asked.

Without hesitation, Raul assured him that this wasn't the case. He was just letting him know how nice of a body she had. Raul led Hakim down the steps.

"How y'all niggas know that this is his mama?" he asked.

"Cause," Raul explained. "Once she saw that we not only had her ass outnumbered in her own house, but we also had them guns on her, she kept saying some shit about how she wasn't going to tell us where her son was."

"Did y'all check the rest of the house to see if his ass was there?" Hakim asked, as they both came to the landing of the basement steps. "You said you saw his car out in the driveway."

"Yeah," Raul told him. "We checked the rest of the house, even the basement. Trust me, man, wasn't nobody else in that house but her. When we came back, they had put the car in the garage."

Raul led Hakim right to the door, where Jayrone stood in his thoughts. Hakim opened the door and smiled, seeing that Marcus' mother was indeed attractive. He wanted to rub his hands together, in a sinister, villain kind of way. He almost felt blessed to have gotten the dude's mother. A man will always come out of hiding for his mother. There was no doubt about that to Hakim.

"Where the fuck is he?" Hakim asked Lorna.

"Like I told them otha niggas," Lorna said, "I ain't tellin' you where he is. I don't give a fuck what you do. I'm not going to tell you shit."

A chuckle slipped out of Hakim's lips as he looked back at Raul and Jayrone. "Aye, niggas," he said. "Why the fuck y'all niggas still standin' there, lookin' dumb and shit? Why ain't this bitch's clothes off yet?"

As soon as Lorna realized what words had just come out of Hakim's mouth, while she had been taking in his very scary presence, Raul and Jayrone were headed back into the bedroom. She resisted at first, but was then pinned down to the bed by one as the other slid her pajamas off. The cold, basement air hit her thick legs as she squirmed. Then, her t-shirt was being ripped away from her body; her bra was undone at the back and came off. Next thing she knew, her panties were being ripped off.

"Damn, she do got some good lookin' pussy, too," Hakim said, licking his lips. He looked up at Lorna. "Why you gotta be like that?" he asked her, smiling. "I'm just try'na get to know you and stuff."

Lorna's arms were let go, allowing her cover her chest and sit up to where she could have her legs closed.

"Fuck you!" Lorna yelled feeling humiliated at being naked. "Fuck you!"

Hakim chuckled, looking back at his boys for a second before looking at Lorna's naked self on the bed. "Y'all hear that?" Hakim asked. "This bitch is tellin' me that she want me to fuck her and maybe that'll get her to tell me where to find this nigga. Ain't that somethin'?"

Raul and Jayrone both nodded at the same time. "Yep," Raul said. Then Jayrone said, "Sure is."

Just then, the two of them watched as Hakim lowered his pants. They couldn't help but see his massive balls swinging, as his manhood was already on its way to its full size. Once Hakim's pants were off, he moved toward the bed. He grabbed Lorna's ankles, both at the same time, and pulled her toward the edge of the bed. She kicked and screamed, but her strength was absolutely no match for someone of Hakim's size. Hakim was practically the same build as Suge Knight.

Within a matter of seconds, Raul and Jayrone were holding Lorna's arms. Tears began to roll down her cheeks as she looked down at Hakim's dick, realizing that she was about to face one of her biggest fears, being raped.

"Just calm down," Hakim said, in a calm voice. "I know you just need some dick and you gon' be feelin' better, won't you? Don't be scared. I got that good dick that I know you'll like."

Hakim pushed himself between Lorna's legs then, inside of her. Lorna shrieked in pain – a shriek that would turn Hakim on even more as he liked to cause the ladies a little bit of pain. Once he was stroking inside of Lorna, with Lorna begging him to stop, he sped up his thrusts. He went hard – full throttle to get his point across. He was putting his back into it, doing everything he could to grudge fuck the mother of the dude that he was looking for.

Once Hakim had finished, he backed away and put his pants back on. "Wait till I find this nigga and he find out that I got some of his mama pussy, that sweet pussy," Hakim said. "He gon' show his face. And when he do, I'mma be ready for him. Bitch, your son shoulda never took my shit – fucked with my money. And he gon' be sorry for fuckin' my chick. Last nigga that did that shit wound up dead."

Raul and Jayrone looked at Hakim, the two of them wondering when they would get their chance to get inside of her. Jayrone was especially eager, as Lorna was just the kind of woman he would go out to clubs and bars to meet—thick in all of the right places.

Hakim led them out of the room and closed the door.

"What we gon' do now?" Raul asked.

Hakim looked at Raul and Jayrone, knowing that he was the smartest out of the three of them. He smiled. "Now?" he said. "Now, all we do is wait."

"Wait?" Jayrone asked, confused.

"Yup," Hakim said, nodding his head. "We just wait. Sooner or later, that nigga is gon' see that his mother is missing, or not answerin' her phone or whatever. And when he do see that, he suddenly gon' show up. We just keep lookin' for that little bitch of his, too. If we can get her, that'd be even better. Aside from that, if all else fails, that nigga Roy will be back. He seem like the kinda nigga that just ain't gon' let go. And that's a'ight with me."

Chapter 6

Kayla woke up abruptly to the sound of the front door closing. It was odd to hear that particular door open because they had parked their car in the back. After dinner, Kayla talked to Marcus for a little while. It was good to know that he was doing okay up in Fort Wayne, and she liked that he still had a little fight in him even with his arm messed up. Nonetheless, Kayla knew that she had to worry about herself. She felt guilty that she was even considering using her looks, her appeal, to her advantage. It was very obvious, especially as the night went on, that this was the very reason that Jonathon had shown any interest in her. The guy simply couldn't hide how much he liked Kayla's body.

Once Kayla registered that the noise that woke her up was the front door opening and closing, she leaned up and peaked out of the blinds. At first, she wasn't sure what she was seeing. However, after a second look, and a little bit of squinting, she could see that her mother had gotten into a car – a car with a man.

Kayla watched, through the front window of Lyesha's house, as her mother appeared to be having a conversation with the guy. Within a matter of minutes, her mother's head looked ahead then back before finally lowering. From then on, all Kayla could see was the silhouette of her mother's hand. It went up and down as the guy in the car leaned his seat back.

Kayla closed the couple of blinds and pushed her head back into her pillow on the couch. There she lay, looking up at the ceiling. She'd always had the suspicion that her mother was doing something strange for a piece of change. However, she'd never actually seen the woman doing it. Seeing her doing it really changed everything – solidified how her mother managed to walk through the door with money but never walked out to go to work.

"Oh my fuckin' God," Kayla said, feeling a little angry. She began to feel mad at herself, for knowing that this man at the library had only helped her to get in line for this job because of her body. *Does that make me a hoe?* Kayla wondered to herself.

Kayla spent the next twenty minutes or so looking up at the ceiling. She knew that she wanted better than this for herself. She hated that her mother would stoop so low as to purposely live that kind of life without even trying to go out and get a job. *At least I'm trying to get a fucking job*, Kayla thought. *At least I'm fucking trying.*

When Rolanda walked through the door, it didn't take her long to see that her daughter was up. Kayla could hear the car pulling off and driving away. Kayla peeked out, not even caring if her mother saw her do it. She then slouched back down into the couch, clearly annoyed by something.

"Somethin' you wanna say?" Rolanda asked, as she shut the door.

"Naw," Kayla said. "You wouldn't be able to talk back anyway."

Rolanda was just taking her coat off and dropping it onto the back of a dining room chair when Kayla had said that. Immediately, she snapped back, turning and looking and her daughter. "What the fuck did you say to me?" Rolanda demanded to know.

"Just forget it," Kayla said, settling back into her pillow. "I already know I'mma be the one to have to get up in the morning and take Latrell and Linell to school. So, I betta get me some sleep so I don't have to worry about oversleeping."

"Fuck all that," Rolanda said, now visibly mad. "What did you mean by that little comment you made? What the fuck you mean I wouldn't be able to talk back? Huh, Kayla?"

"Mama," Kayla said. "I looked out the window and saw what you was doin'."

"And what did you think you saw me doin'?" Rolanda asked.

Just then, Kayla could pick up on the fact that her mother was a little tipsy. It dawned on her that while she and the guy were talking, a bottle must have been going back and forth between the two of them. Kayla's head shook, without her realizing it.

"Mama," Kayla said. "I saw you. I saw your head go down in that nigga's lap. I saw it goin' up and down."

"Okay," Rolanda said, feeling a little backed into a corner. "What you want me to say? At least I'm the one goin' out here try'na get this money, any money of any kind. You just a usin' ass little bitch."

Kayla sat up, ready to go off. Her mother was purposely keeping her voice low as to not wake up anyone upstairs. Just as Kayla was about to say something, Rolanda cut her off.

"And one more thing, Kayla, in case you done forgot," Rolanda said, swaying a little bit. "We only here because of your ass," she said. "If you wouldn't have been fuckin' round with that no good nigga Marcus, we wouldn't even be in this mess. So don't be talkin' about me cause you lookin' real stupid at this point if you ask me."

Rolanda shook her head, looked down at the floor and laughed. The irony was just too much for her. "The nigga done started some shit that he can't finish," Rolanda said. "And he done left this bitch," she pointed at Kayla, "in Indianapolis while he is carried away somewhere like he some damn fuckin' royalty or somethin', and leave his chick to basically hide and run for her life, with her family. And here she is, complainin' when her mama is at least doin' somethin' to fix the situation. She over there sittin' on her ass, doin' nothing."

Kayla resented what her mother said, rising to her feet. Even if her mother was drunk, she took every word she said to be truly reflective of what she thought. At this point in her life, Kayla had already learned that a good way to get the truth out of somebody is to get them drunk. The fact that her mother was clearly tipsy, and maybe even a little dizzy, told Kayla that she was finding out what she really thought.

"And where the fuck you goin', Miss Thang?" Rolanda asked, noticing how Kayla had stood up like she was really going to do something.

"Outta here," Kayla said, walking toward her mother. "I gotta get outta here. My mother is a damn prostitute, suckin' dick for money."

Just then, Rolanda stopped Kayla dead in her tracks as she was trying to enter the dining room. Rolanda reached her arm out, gripping the doorway framework. Kayla looked down, breathing so hard through her nostrils that her mother could feel the air hitting her forearm. Rolanda snickered, finding it funny how mad her daughter could get when she really had no right to be mad to begin with.

"I swear," Rolanda said, shaking her head. "You a piece of work, you little bitch. All this shit is your fault."

"Move out my way," Kayla said, pushing her mother's arm.

Once Rolanda's arm gave way to Kayla's force, she had truly been pushed to her edge. There was no way, no matter whose house they were staying in, that she was going to allow this child to treat her like that. No way, not happening.

Rolanda, with a stare that could cut through a big glass building downtown, zeroed in on Kayla's head, just as the back of it was to her. Kayla had leaned down and appeared to be getting some clothes out of her bag. With a heavy hand, and a pumped arm, Rolanda swung as hard as she could. The palm of her hand collided with the side of Kayla's head, causing Kayla to fall to the side and into the wall.

Immediately, with the side of her head stinging, Kayla was in full-on self-defense mode. She looked at her mother as if she was any other chick out in the streets. The woman was begging for it, so Kayla was going to give it to her.

Without even thinking, Kayla raised her fists and struck her mother. Within a matter of seconds, they had grabbed hold of one another's hair. Hair came out here, then fell there. At moments one would grip the other's clothes. Over the next few minutes, all the frustration the two of them had been going through was being let off of their chests and onto the other one.

Kayla was tired of her mother basically being like a teenage girl in the house, leaving her to take care of her younger brother and sister. Rolanda was tired of Kayla thinking that she could just talk to her mother in any way she felt like, at any moment. The mother and daughter tore into one another, first pushing into the dining room table, then into the wall, and eventually the living room. Just as they were pushing one another toward the television and entertainment system, some lights flipped on. It was Lyesha. She had rushed down the stairs, hearing the two rustling about. Behind her stood the sleepy eyed Latrell and Linell. Both of them had woken up to see what was causing the commotion.

Just as Rolanda was about to really go in on her daughter, Lyesha was breaking the two of them up.

"Break it up, you two," she said, her hair wrapped up. "Break it up. Stop! Stop! Stop!"

Rolanda and Kayla pulled away from one another. They both looked as if they had just gotten into a hardcore street fight. Instead, it had all taken place in the dining room and living room of Lyesha's house.

Just as Lyesha was trying to figure out what was going on, Kayla went ahead and slid into some clothes. She pulled some gray sweatpants up over her pajama pants; she slid a cut sweater down over her t-shirt. Once she'd slid into her coat, Rolanda been bombarding her with questions, like asking her where she was going and if she needed her ass to be whooped some more. Kayla was so mad she knew she'd better just ignore her mother. At the rate of how things were going, they were close to having to call the police. For a split second, Kayla felt like she didn't love her mother anymore. She pushed through the living room, ignoring both her mother and Lyesha. She picked her phone up off of the couch and headed out of the front door.

Out on the porch, a cold wind greeted Kayla. She wasn't quite sure where she was going, especially at this time of night. However, she knew that she had to get away from what was her temporary home. She didn't even know if she'd be able to go back and go to sleep tonight, knowing that she and her mother were sharing the front room.

Kayla did what she only saw as the sensible thing to do. She headed toward 38th Street. She hoped that the White Castles, which she knew was open twenty-four hours, would still have its doors open. For the next two blocks, she used the snow beneath her feet and the bitter wind making the sides of her face sting to calm down. She was in luck because White Castles' lobby was indeed open for business. As she approached the intersection of 38th and Keystone, she could see that people were inside.

Kayla crossed the busy, wide street and hurried into the White Castles lobby. Once inside, she was incredibly happy to be warm. The two blocks from Lyesha's house had seemed almost like a mile from how cold it was. She sat down in a booth, telling the lady behind the glassed-in counter that she was going to decide what to eat in a few minutes. Once seated, Kayla looked down the street – down Keystone. She knew that she didn't want to go back to that house.

Out of instinct, Kayla pulled her phone out and set it on the table. After several seconds of thinking who she could text, she found herself back on the text message from Jonathon. She read over it again, shaking her head as he seemed like someone who could really help her, especially in this time. If she could get this job, her life would be a lot better. She didn't have Marcus around now to take her out to nice restaurants or buy her things at the mall. These were all things she'd have to do for herself.

"Fuck, I need this job," Kayla said to herself, quietly. She replied to Jonathon's text message, cringing as she did so, *That would be cool*. She rationalized to herself that getting with Jonathon might not be all that bad of an idea. Technically, for right now, she was single, or at least that's how she tried to reason it. Furthermore, Marcus was only doing what he had to do. Kayla thought of her situation in the same manner. She was only doing what she had to do.

Kayla wasn't even sure that what she had responded to Jonathon would get a response. It was kind of late. And with him being a professional kind of man, it wasn't likely that he'd be up through the night. Kayla simply relaxed back into her seat, eventually looking through her small wallet, which had been in her coat pocket. As long as she was at White Castles, she might as well have a little dinner.

Once Kayla sat back down after ordering some food, her phone vibrated. It was a response from Jonathon. His somewhat dorky, round self popped up in Kayla's mind as she opened the text message: *Wyd tonight?*

Kayla was instantly nervous. She responded, *just chilling*.

After several texts going back and forth between Kayla and Jonathon, Kayla had agreed for him to come pick her up. It turned out that he didn't stay all that far from where Kayla was staying. Once he found that out, he offered to come swoop her up. She'd told him that she'd gotten into it with her mother and didn't want to go home.

Within twenty minutes, Jonathon had pulled up out in the parking lot. Kayla was impressed with his car – black, sleek, and clearly new – even if she wasn't really all that turned on by him as a person. Kayla left the restaurant and hopped into the front passenger seat. Jonathon looked at her, his eyes looking bold in his glasses.

"You okay over there?" Jonathon asked Kayla. He reached over and rubbed her thigh. "You got in the car and looked like you had seen a ghost or something."

Jonathon pulled off and headed down 38th Street, back the way he'd come. Kayla got comfortable in her seat while still being sure to keep her guard up. She looked over at Jonathon and smiled. "Oh, no," she said. "It's not like that. I was just cold and a little upset is all."

"You wanna tell me what happened with your mother that got you out here this time of night like this?" Jonathon asked, really sounding comforting.

Kayla looked over at him. "Oh, just we ain't been real cool lately," she answered. "A lot of shit is going on between us. I just really hope that I get this job so I ain't got to be bothered with her ass no more."

"You will," Jonathon said, smiling.

Soon enough, Jonathon was turning the car into a more upscale apartment complex on Binford Blvd. The complex was surrounded by woods. The cars in the parking lot even looked better. Quickly, Kayla got comfortable, never having been to an apartment complex like this. Jonathon walked her inside and sat her in his living room. Kayla was a little nervous, but Jonathon had been very nice to her so far. Plus, she really liked his place as it was certainly better than sleeping on Lyesha's couch.

"Relax," Jonathon insisted. "Relax. So, let me ask you, do you drink wine?"

Kayla shrugged. She'd never really had the chance to have any wine. Sure, she would have a little bit here and there, or at family functions. However, she didn't really know much about it or any names. "Sure," Kayla said, sliding out of her coat. "I'll have some."

Within minutes, Jonathon had poured a couple of glasses of wine and came back into his living room to sit down. Kayla surveyed the place, noticing how the man had quite a few plants placed about. His furniture was nice, with a couple of pieces being antique. Even as they talked about this and that, Kayla could not help but feel a little guilty. *What am I doing here?* She thought. She thought about how mad Marcus would be if he knew what was going on.

Kayla kept up a smile, sipping the wine and actually liking the taste a little bit. "Well, I do thank you for introducing me to the human resources lady," Kayla said, in response to a comment that Jonathon had made about being in the right place at the right time.

Jonathon rubbed Kayla's thick thighs, his hands clearly getting a good feel. "No problem, no problem," he said. "There was just something about you that told me that you were stressed out, and I started to think about what I could do to help you out." He smiled. "I didn't mean to offend you or anything, just trying to let you know what I was thinking."

"Did you only help me because of my body?" Kayla came out and asked.

Jonathon nearly choked, as he was taken off guard by Kayla's question. However, he knew that she was on to him as her body was what first caught his attention.

"I'd be lying if I told you that I didn't notice it," Jonathon said, his eyes lowering towards Kayla's legs and backside.

"You certainly have it going on, and have a good mind about you."

Kayla felt the wine starting to kick in. No longer was she nervous. Rather, she simply carried on a conversation with Jonathon. She'd never been with a man who was as suave and professional as him. Sure, he wasn't really all that handsome, especially compared to Marcus. However, he was slowly seeming okay to Kayla.

They continued sipping their wine. "I had a feeling you was lookin'," Kayla said.

"Sorry if that's a problem," Jonathon said. "But you are very pretty. In fact, you're probably the prettiest woman I've seen come up in that library in a long time."

Kayla laughed, seeing the hint of desperation in Jonathon's eyes. She kind of liked how just her looks was enough to get a man to show her some attention. She still struggled with what he meant by his text message earlier. There was something about their interaction that seemed very professional to Kayla, and she really wasn't sure where it was going.

"So, are you interested?" Jonathon came out and asked Kayla. "I mean, in making a little on the side of the library job. Like I said, I can put in a good word for you tomorrow to at least get you in real good with the hiring lady. But, umm." Jonathon hesitated. "I'm also open to giving you a chance to get a little something extra." Just then, Jonathon pulled a wad of money out of his pocket and looked up at Kayla.

Kayla was a bit surprised. She saw quite a bit of money in Jonathon's hand, but nothing off the Richter scale or anything. She thought about it for a second, wondering what exactly he wanted.

"So, what you try'na do with me?" Kayla asked.

"You know," Jonathon said, clearly starting to feel a little nervous. "Just, you know, when you got some free time. You can hit me up or whatever and come over and chill with me for a little bit. I ain't into no kinky, stupid shit."

"So you just wanna fuck?" Kayla asked.

"Well, um…" Jonathon said. "We can spend a little time together if you want."

Just then, Kayla couldn't help but lower her eyes down to Jonathon's private area. With how he was sitting on the couch, she didn't see much of a bulge. While he may not have been the cream of the crops when it came to the looks department, he certainly wasn't the kind of guy who couldn't land a woman no matter how hard he tried. Kayla wondered what was up, and why he was up for paying a chick to basically be his pussy-on-demand.

Kayla continued on with the conversation. She and Jonathon worked out a deal, for lack of a better word. Eventually, Jonathon had gotten up and walked across the room to dim the lights. Kayla finished her glass of wine, feeling just the least bit tipsy, and certainly feeling better by just being in a better environment like Jonathon's place.

Jonathon came back over and sat next to Kayla. Within a matter of seconds, he had moved closer to her and was kissing up her neck. Kayla giggled, trying to get herself in the mood to let Jonathon push up on her and get inside of her. She still wasn't comfortable with the entire situation. Even though she was a little buzzed, she felt as if she was doing something dirty by fucking this man she'd just met. However, she also knew that by giving him what he wanted – or what he needed – he would be more likely to make sure that she got hooked up with the job at the library.

Kayla did not move. Rather, she allowed it to happen, thinking about the money and what a different it would make in her life. Upon seeing that she wasn't resisting, Jonathon went as far as fondling her chest and making comments about her body. When he went in for a kiss, Kayla clearly hesitated before going along with what he wanted. She stood up, knowing that she could probably do the same things she did for Marcus with Jonathon and he would like it.

In front of Jonathon, Kayla dropped her pants. Quickly, he had leaned forward and slapped her ass before rubbing his face in it. Once Kayla got completely naked, she motioned for Jonathon to pull his pants down. In a hurry, he did just that. Kayla, with slight disappointment, lowered herself down to her knees as she watched Jonathon's manhood pop out of his pants. Wrapping her hand around it, she could see right away that it was not only significantly less than Marcus', but it was also clearly shorter than a dollar bill.

Kayla gave him the best head that she felt like giving at that moment. Several minutes into it, Jonathon had pulled her head up out of his lap and was guiding her back to his bedroom. With his clothes off, Kayla could see that he was not in shape as she had thought. And nothing turned her on about his dick at all, especially when she could mentally compare it to Marcus.

Nonetheless, Kayla went with the flow. Jonathan gently placed her onto his bed and grabbed some condoms. Soon enough, Kayla was lying under his grunting body, as he thrust into her in the missionary position. While she waited on him to finish, she could only stare at the ceiling. It wasn't long before the buzz from the wine was wearing off. Reality was sinking in, like salt to a fresh wound. A tear rolled down Kayla's eyes, with Jonathon's head buried next to her head, grunting. His body was becoming increasingly sweaty, to the point where Kayla wanted to use her legs to push him and his blubbery body off of her.

Once Jonathon had released himself, he turned over onto his back next to Kayla. He told her how good her pussy was, and, not to mention, just how pretty she was. Kayla took the compliments for what they were before going back to looking at the ceiling. Soon enough, Jonathon was snoring, leaving Kayla to think in the dark. She was in this strange man's apartment, doing what she felt she had to do to get a little money, if nothing else. Hopefully her actions would lead to this job. Being in hiding was nothing to play about, and Kayla hated that she was in this situation.

***

When Kayla woke up in the morning, at the time she might normally get up to get her brother and sister ready, she woke up Jonathon as well. As long as she was up, she was going to try her hardest to get back to Lyesha's house. She couldn't count on her mother to get up and get them ready. And the last thing they needed right then was for the truancy officers to be breathing down their neck because of the kids missing so much school.

On the drive back to the White Castles, Kayla had basically reconciled with her feelings of guilt. It was what it was at this point. She could only hope that she really would get a job at the library. From what Jonathon told her, it really did sound like a good job to have. The little money on the side wouldn't hurt either, especially since Jonathon seemed to lead a relatively low-key life. There was no sign of any other chick being at his place, and he sure didn't look like he was involved in any sort of street life activities.

Kayla got out of the car in the White Castles parking lot, with Jonathon telling her that he would put in a good word when he got to work later on. Kayla thanked him and began walking down the street. She had a little pep in her step, not only because she had to get home for Latrell and Linell, but also because she had a little money in her pocket.

Chapter 7

Roy was fuming all the way home from his sister Lorna's house. On the way to his house, he hit up Juan and Brandon. He asked them if they could come through to talk real quick. Roy waited for one of them to get off work so that they both could ride over together. It was very obvious to both Juan and Brandon that Roy was royally pissed off about something. They inched into the living room, took off their coats, and sat down.

"Damn, Roy," Juan said, seeing from across the room that steam was practically blowing out of the man's ears. "What's got you all fucked up?"

Roy laughed, loving how the younger generation was so full of youth and culture. "I went and had a little meeting with Hakim today," he told them then looked away.

Brandon and Juan looked at one another, both knowing what that meant. Juan, who was the taller of the two, stood up. "And what that nigga say?" he asked Roy. "What he say, Roy?"

"It ain't good," Roy said. "He definitely gon' keep comin' after Marcus, y'all. I could see it in his eyes. He gon' keep on comin' after Marcus."

Roy went into detail, telling Brandon and Juan everything about his meeting earlier at Hakim's house. Just as he was about to go into detail and talk about how he'd pulled up at his sister's house to find Marcus' car in the driveway, he stopped himself. He remembered that Brandon and Juan weren't supposed to know where Marcus was and that he was up in Fort Wayne. He had already broken his promise to Lorna by talking to Marcus. He certainly wasn't going to break the promise of not telling his boys, who she was so suspicious of. Instead, he steered the conversation back to Hakim specifically.

Juan was all worked up. "Man, fuck this shit!" he said. "I don't care what y'all say or what y'all do! We gotta get this nigga before he get us. I swear, man, I don't even know why you ain't just kill his ass right then and there when he was makin' a threat on your nephew life like that."

Roy stood up, ready to teach this young dude something. "Listen here," he said. "You just can't go doin' whatever you wanna do, whenever you wanna do it. That's what's wrong with you young niggas nowadays. You too quick to react. With all them doors that nigga had in his house, for all I know, there could'a been ten, twenty niggas up in there just waitin' on my ass to fuck up so they could pump me full with bullets. Think about it, Juan. Hakim knew that as I was comin', and based on some of the stuff that he was sayin', he already knew that I was Marcus' uncle even before we got to that point in the conversation. Trust me, nigga. He prolly had niggas watchin' me and shit. I swear, as I was walkin' out to my car and shit, I felt like somebody was watchin' me, probably from them damn basement windows or some shit, fuck if I know."

"So, what are you thinkin' we do?" Brandon came out and asked. "When we gon' kill this nigga so we ain't gotta worry about this shit no more?"

Roy, surprised that Brandon had said that considering he was generally the quieter of the two, look across the room and sat back down on the couch. "Tomorrow night," he said, confidently. "I already talked to a nigga bout gettin' a couple pieces with silencers. Hakim's property is so wooded and shit, not to mention the house is backed up off of the road. I see so many weak points and ways that we can roll up on that nigga. All we gotta do is jump over that fence."

"There's a fuckin' fence and shit we gotta jump over?" Juan said, clearly sounding annoyed by that idea. "Is you fuckin' serious?"

"And it sounded like there was dog there, prolly a Pit Bull or something," Roy said. "It was down in the basement or somewhere. When I got there, Hakim had this big booty chick walking out of the kitchen and heading to the bedroom, cleaning up something. She gotta go too."

"Wait a sec," Juan said. "You talkin' bout runnin' up in there and just killin' every damn body."

Roy shrugged. "The only way we gon' get this nigga off our back is if we kill his ass," he said. "You and me both know that. But we also gotta keep the law off our back. Now, they prolly already lookin' at his ass, but I don't know and don't wanna know. I wanna run up in that shit and kill his ass and whoever else is there. Take all they goddamn cell phone and throw that shit in a ravine or creek nearby. That way, they can't even call the damn police. When we leave that shit, I want it to have been a quiet massacre. That'll be the only way that we not only get Hakim's ass and kill him, but we also kill any witnesses or people who may have seen me, or us, there at all. Sorry, but they gotta go. Collateral damage is how I see it."

Brandon and Juan looked at one another. "We went and bought some shit too," Brandon said.

"Yeah, a couple guns from this nigga we know over on East Washington Street," Juan said.

Roy asked what kind of guns they were, with Juan explaining the types. When he finished, his head was shaking. "Look, niggas," he said. "We gotta do shit in such a way that we ain't drawin' attention to ourselves. We gotta pull up and get our ass in there. In and out, quick. Shooting whoever gets in the way, except any kids, if there are any kids even there. If this shit goes right, Marcus gon' be okay and we gon' be okay. Everybody havin' to look over they shoulder cause of this shit. That mean that the obvious answer is to get ready for any and everything that you havin' to look over your shoulder for. Just as simple as that."

Brandon and Juan nodded, totally understanding the wisdom that Roy was dropping on them right then. They went on to roll a blunt and share it while Roy went over just how Hakim's property was laid out.

"What about the dog?" Juan asked. "You know that dog gon' make noise as soon as we step on the property."

"I know," Roy said. "That dog gon' be the way we get their attention and let them know that we there without knowing where. I'm thinkin' that two of us cause the dog to bark because we comin' from the front – that can be you two. Then, the other one, me, finds a way to come out of them woods and sneak up at the back of the house. Knowing that nigga, he will prolly be so worried about what is going on at the front of his house, that the back will become a blind spot. That is when I get up in that shit from the back, down on the basement that lets out. What I want you two niggas to do is when you know Hakim and whoever else is comin' toward the front of the house, to see what the dog is barking about, just start shooting up his shit. With silencers on the gun, all anyone is gonna here out there is glass snapping and breaking. Shit, that nigga's front yard is fuckin' wooded that I seriously doubt nobody gon' see shit go down from the road out front."

Juan smiled. He liked that he felt like he was in on some James Bond shit. Sure, he'd done a couple of criminal activities before that required some beforehand planning, just like when they hit a couple of licks on some houses out in the suburb. However, this was different because they were going up in there to leave any and everybody cold on the floor.

"That shit is smart," Brandon said. "Create a diversion so you can sneak up on the back of them."

"Exactly," Roy said, nodding his head. "Now you see what I'm talkin' about. Whatever we gotta do, we gotta get rid of Hakim and his boys – them niggas he sending to do his dirty work and shit. Like I said, get rid of whatever you havin' to look over your shoulder for. Plus, I got a bad feeling that we gotta do this the sooner the better. Hakim seem like he got a little bit of energy or whatever invested in this, meaning that all day tomorrow we'd betta be watchin' our shit in case he got somebody after our asses because we know Marcus."

***

Later on that night, Brandon and Juan were in the car with one another and were headed back home. There was a thick, somewhat tense silence between the two of them that might not normally be there. Eventually, Juan broke the ice. What had been on his mind could very well be on his boy Brandon's mind. He was just going to come on out and ask.

"We really gon' go kill that nigga tomorrow, ain't we?" Juan said.

Brandon looked over. "Yeah," he said. "We gotta do it."

Juan nodded. "Fuck yeah, we do," he said. "You heard what Roy said. That nigga Hakim is really out here and doin' whatever he gotta do to get Marcus. This some fucked up shit."

"Well, Marcus ain't have to fuck the dude's bitch," Brandon said. "What the fuck was he thinkin' when he did that shit? Ain't no way that something like that could turn out good."

"You right about that," Juan said. "I can't wait to just run up in that shit tomorrow."

"You think about the innocent people, though?" Brandon asked. "You know, the people who really ain't have shit to do with this."

"Who you rather go? Them or us?" Juan asked, as if the answer was obvious.

"Yeah, I feel you on that," Brandon said. "I'm just sayin', I hope we ain't gotta go up in there mass shootin' and shit. I wanted to say to Roy that we needed to find a way to just get Hakim."

"But what about his boys?" Juan asked. "Them niggas he got goin' around the city, scarin' niggas and shit? What about them?"

"Y'all fuckin' overexaggerating about that shit," Brandon said, looking over at his boy Juan. "You know them niggas just doin' whatever the fuck they doin' to get the money. Once the money stop comin', they ain't gon be makin' no more moves. They focus is gon be on findin' the next big-time nigga to go do his dirty work for a little money. Killing Hakim really is all we gotta do and shit. I don't know about all this mass killin' shit."

"We don't even know how many niggas gon be up in that house," Juan pointed out. "Roy said that when he was there he saw it was just Roy and a chick. What are the chances that his two niggas would even be there?"

Brandon leaned his head to the side, realizing that Juan was making a good point. "I'll be glad when this nigga dead and shit, though," he said. "Like Roy said, we ain't gon have to be lookin' over our backs and shit. I ain't been gettin' the same sleep I used to be gettin'. I keep thinkin' I hear something and I'm jumping up and ready to put some bullets in some niggas if I have to."

"Yeah, I feel you on that, my nigga," Juan said. "I'll be glad when this nigga is dead tomorrow too. One more day and hopefully all this shit will be over with. Speakin' of that, did Marcus text you back."

Brandon shrugged. "Yeah, he did a little," he responded. "I mean, the nigga sounded like he really wasn't try'na say a whole lot and shit."

"Yeah, that's the same shit I was thinkin'," Juan said. "When I text the nigga, it took him for fuckin' ever to text a nigga back. Then…then he really ain't have much to say. I sent him a message tellin' him that we could come through and see him whenever he's ready and shit. He ain't hit me back."

Juan and Brandon finished the rest of their ride home talking back and forth. They were both starting to feel like Marcus was holding some other shit back. However, neither of them wanted to come out and say it. Rather, they kept their thoughts to themselves and headed into the apartment building doors.

Chapter 8

Just as Kayla thought would happen, she wound up having to take Latrell and Linell to school. When she walked through the door in the morning, after spending the night with Jonathon, everything felt a little different. She couldn't help but think that just eight or nine hours before, she'd been involved in a full-blown fight with her mother.

Just as Kayla was walking Latrell and Linell out of the back door to get into the car, Rolanda woke up.

"Kayla," she said, loud enough for her to hear from the front room.

Kayla, reluctantly, turned around in the kitchen and stepped in front of the doorway, now looking at her mother. "What is it?" she asked.

"Because of your little show you put on last night, hittin' you mother back and shit, Lyesha said we gotta be gon' within a few more days if we gon' be actin' like that," Rolanda said, snapping her neck to the side.

Kayla nodded, giving her mother slanted eyes. "Okay," she said. "I'm taking your children to school. I'll be back in a little bit."

On that note, Kayla turned around and walked out of the back door. The entire ride to school from Lyesha's house on the east side was only a big reminder for Kayla. It took her three times as long to get to the school, with most of the way consisting of Latrell and Linell talking amongst themselves in the backseat. As soon as she dropped them off at the school doors and waved goodbye to them, she hopped onto her phone and called her girl Myesha. She needed to talk and she needed to talk badly.

"Hello?" Myesha answered, sounding fully alert.

"Wassup, girl?" Kayla said. "It's me."

"Girl, how you been doin'?" Myesha asked. "I been thinkin' about you and stuff."

"Girl, I'm okay," Kayla said. Even then, however, she just couldn't hide the anguish in her voice.

Myesha came right out and said, "Girl, why you lyin' to me? I can tell that you not all right. Why are you telling me that you are, Kayla? What happened? What's going on?"

"Where you at right now?" Kayla asked. "I just dropped Latrell and Linell off at the school, so I'm not too far from the house."

"Girl, that's wassup," Myesha said. "I'm actually at home. My mother just left to go somewhere or another, I don't know. You know she always stay busy doing something. You want to come on over right now?"

Kayla agreed to coming over and told Myesha that she'd be over in five minutes. In just that amount of time, she was walking up Myesha's walkway, just a block up from her own. As Kayla stepped inside of the house, she had no idea who was parked in a car down the block from her and that there were eyes watching her.

Myesha gave Kayla a big hug, which was just what Kayla needed at that moment. "Girl, how have you been?" Myesha asked.

Kayla just shook her head. "My life is a fuckin' mess, girl," Kayla said. "Everything is just fuckin' fallin' apart."

Kayla filled Myesha in on Marcus going out of town. She then moved on to meeting the man at the library who was trying to help her get a job working in the call center department. Of course, she had to fill Myesha in on getting into a full-blown fight with her mother last night. This story, naturally, led to Kayla's deal with Jonathon. Kayla apologized if she left anything out, but she'd really had a rough couple of days.

"Shit," Myesha said, clearly taken aback by what she was hearing. "I'm sorry, girl," she said. "But that is some fucked up shit you got goin'."

"And Marcus is talkin' about try'na come back down here and kill the dude," Kayla added. "His uncle out there doin' somethin' or another now, so we'll see what happens with this shit."

"This sound like some fuckin' mafia shit, girl," Myesha said. The two of them sat next to one another on the couch in her mother's living room. Myesha, who wasn't blessed so much in the looks department as Kayla, was always so comforting when people needed advice from her. "Who did Marcus get involved with that would cause all of this shit to happen, Kayla?"

"Some nigga," Kayla said, appearing very angry. "Some nigga named Hakim or somethin'. I don't know. Never even heard of the nigga."

"Hakim?" Myesha asked then taking a moment to think. "I don't think I know who that is either. So, you really have gone out and gotten you a sugar daddy to help you out."

"I had to, girl," Kayla said. "I felt like if I didn't go along, that, you know, he would not put in a good word for me to get the job."

"From what it sounds like, it would be better than flipping burgers at McDonald's," Myesha said.

"Girl, I know," Kayla said. "I felt so low when I was filling out them online job applications for fast food restaurants. I was praying to God that they didn't call me, so I'd at least have a reason to go rob banks."

"Girl, you betta not be robbin' no banks," Myesha said. "Last thing you need right now is to be on the news. If this Hakim person is as crazy as he sounds like, it sounds like you working in the basement at the library just might be where you need to be. You don't know how long it is before Marcus, or his Uncle, will actually be able to stop this dude. Plus, by this, a whole bunch of stuff can happen, as you can see. Look at the few days you've had." Myesha shook her head.

Kayla looked at Myesha, squinting her eyes. "Okay, girl," she said, sarcastically. "You ain't got to go shittin' on me too hard, do you?"

"Girl, you know I didn't mean it like that," Myesha insisted. "I was just sayin'. I mean, is this Jonathon guy at least cute? Is he worth fuckin' a little bit so you can get what you need?"

"It ain't what he look like that's botherin' me," Kayla said, realizing that she'd forgotten to fill Myesha in on how she's seen her mother step out of Lyesha's house last night to go give a man some head in a car out front. She filled Myesha in, quickly, seeing the shocked look on her face. "So, yeah,"

Kayla added. "That's why I feel guilty about it, but guilty because I don't get why it doesn't bother me. The very thing I was just gettin' on my mama for..."

"Is the very thing you fell into that could really help you out," Myesha said, finishing Kayla's sentence.

Kayla nodded. "Exactly," she said. "But, I mean, this Jonathon dude doesn't seem like he's the crazy type of whatever. He just seems like a low-key, professional dude that's willing to have a little arrangement. When he was on top of me, I swear I couldn't wait to get done."

"But you felt all better when you got the money, didn't you?" Myesha asked.

"Wouldn't say that I felt better," Kayla said. "I just felt compensated. We need this money so bad right now. We can't go back to the house, ain't none of us got no income, and my mama told me when I was leavin' earlier to take Latrell and Linell to school that Lyesha may want us to be gettin' on up outta there in like three days or somethin'."

"Well," Myesha said. "If you all are having fights and stuff in her living room, then I could definitely see why she'd want something like that. But, what I wanna know is, what you gon' do if you don't get the job at the library? Are you going to keep the little side thing with this Jonathon person or what?"

Kayla looked at her girl Myesha and shook her head. "I don't know," she answered, knowing that she hadn't even thought of that.

Myesha got up and lead Kayla into the kitchen. Once she heard that Kayla hadn't had anything to eat yet, she insisted on making her a little breakfast. Myesha was hungry as well, so it would be killing two birds with one stone.

In no time at all, Myesha had prepared some pancakes, scrambled eggs, and a few strips of bacon. She and Kayla sat across from one another at the wooden kitchen table, chit chatting about this and that.

"You really think they gon' have to kill this guy, Hakim, to make him stop coming after Marcus?" Myesha asked.

"That just seems to be what Marcus was saying," Kayla said. "Girl, it had been a while since I heard him get that angry. I could tell that just talkin' about that shit was making him real mad. I didn't even wanna interrupt."

"But to the point where he's going to try to come back here, from wherever he is, and actually kill the person?" Myesha asked, wanting clarification. "Excuse me, girl, but that sound like some bold shit that he'd better be having a plan for if he really thinks that it's going to work. If the guy's got a couple of crazy niggas with guns going around and terrorizing families and stuff to get to one other person that ain't even in this family, then it sound like he the kinda person that is going to be prepared for whatever Marcus tries to pull."

"I know," Kayla said. "I just hope that his uncle Roy is really doin' somethin' to make all this shit stop. I hate havin' to look over my shoulder when I go places and stuff, girl. It don't feel good."

"You made sure that nobody followed you here, right?" Myesha asked.

Kayla nodded. "Yeah," she said. "I was watchin' all the way from my mama's friend's house to the school, then over here. I swear, girl. I would never bring any sort of drama or bullshit to your house. When I was comin' over here, I made sure to keep a look out for seein' that black car, or any car, following behind me for too long. Luckily, the streets wasn't all that crowded, so I could see the different lanes and actually look further back."

Myesha went back to eating her breakfast, feeling more relaxed. Once they both finished eating, Myesha took the plates, cleaned them off in the sinks, then led Kayla back into the living room.

"I don't wanna hold you up too much more," Kayla said. "I was just stoppin' by. I betta go on and get back down to the library so I can fill out job applications and shit, just in case this library thing don't work out. Plus, I don't wanna be home with my mama at this point. I gotta go back over there to change my clothes, since I really ain't get much sleep last night, and head on downtown. I'd rather sit anywhere than be sitting up in the house with her ass. You know she don't go nowhere. All she do is sit there and probably watch TV."

"Okay, girl," Myesha said, getting an idea. "I actually need to go to the library too. My professor gave us this assignment where we can only use sources that are books and stuff. I can actually meet you down there, whenever you get there, and you can work on what you gotta work on and I can do me."

Kayla stood up, liking the idea as she grabbed her coat and her keys. Within a matter of minutes, she was heading out the door, glad that she and her girl Myesha had found a way to hang out while also getting things done. Plus, hanging out with Myesha would be one good way to loosen her up. Kayla had already made up her mind that she would call Marcus, later on when she was leaving the library.

When Kayla pulled out of her parking spot, she didn't notice the green van pulling out of a parking spot that was not too far down from Kayla's house. She zigzagged through her neighborhood, never thinking a thought of the green mini-van that remained so many blocks behind her at all times. This would prove to be a crucial mishap in her hiding, and she didn't even know it.

***

Raul was on the phone with Hakim as he drove the van. To his side sat Jayrone. He watched the car Kayla drove, which was a very common red, not-too-new model car.

"Yeah, man," Raul said to Hakim. "We followin' her now to see where she headed. We just so happened to be sittin' up by her place when we saw her come out of another house down the street. We saw which house it was that she came out of, so I wonder if she and the little kidos are staying in there. Plus, that mama of hers. That bitch can get it."

"Just chill out, nigga," Hakim said. "Keep doin' what you doin' and keep on followin' her. Let's see where she goes — where she leads us to. Don't go runnin' up in nowhere either. All that won't be necessary. Just see where she goes for now and call me back when you have somethin' again."

"A'ight," Raul said, hanging up the phone. He looked over at Jayrone. "He wants us to sit on her. He really try'na do everything he can to draw this nigga Marcus out."

"Yeah, man, I know," Jayrone said. "I know I'mma never fuck none of his bitches. I wanted to run up in that room last night with the nigga's mama so bad. I'd leave that pussy sore if Hakim gave me the chance." He shook his head. "The bitch just don't know."

Raul chuckled. "Then your ass gon' be swimmin' with the fishes in the canal too," he said, mimicking an Italian accent. He looked back at the road ahead, making sure to keep his eyes on Marcus' girlfriend. "Don't think for one second that nigga won't do the same thing to us that he try'na do to this nigga Marcus. Don't think that for one fuckin' second."

Raul remained rather close behind Kayla, following her all the way over to the east side. Once she pulled into the alley behind a house on Keystone, Raul pulled into a parking spot on the next street over. From where he was parked, he could see between two houses to see which house Kayla was going into. He smiled, looking at his boy Jayrone, as he picked up the phone and called Hakim back. Hakim would be very interested to know where they had followed Marcus' girlfriend to, and with doing such, they might have just found where he is.

Chapter 9

Kayla had a decent day at the library. She had gone back to Lyesha's house, changed into some better clothes without getting into it with her mother, and headed downtown. Just as the two of them had planned, Kayla and Myesha met up at the library. They sat side by side while Myesha worked on some things for school and Kayla applied for jobs. She needed to be prepared in case, for whatever reason, the job with the library just didn't come through.

The two of them finished up just before three o'clock and walked out to the library parking garage. They walked together as they zigzagged through the parking garage, until they both came to their cars. Myesha promised Kayla that she would call her later on, with Kayla promising to keep her girl updated if anything new happened, which she prayed to God wouldn't. When Kayla got into her car and pulled off, she headed up to Latrell and Linell's school.

On the ride up there, Kayla started to think about how she wasn't being completely honest with Myesha. For whatever reason, she felt a little guilty at not telling her best friend where she was staying. She knew that there was just no way, in the whole world, that Myesha would ever tell anyone. In fact, Kayla could see just how much Myesha cared about her and her situation just by the look in her eyes. That'd been so comforting to Kayla, knowing that she had one person she could trust in this entire world.

When Kayla pulled up at the school, she waited, alongside the mothers and fathers of other children. After about ten minutes, she could hear the school's bell ring from inside. Within a matter of minutes, Latrell and Linell came walking out. They practically bounced up and down with how they walked, Linell shielding her face from some of the snow that had been caught up in the wind.

Latrell and Linell climbed into the car. Both of them said *hey* to their sister as she pulled out from the sidewalk and headed down the street.

"Wassup y'all?" Kayla asked. It was very clear to Latrell and Linell that Kayla was in a better mood than she'd been in earlier that morning.

"So," Latrell said. "Why were you and Mama fighting?"

Kayla cringed. She really didn't want that incident to be brought up. However, she knew that when it came to a couple of nine-year-old kids, it would all be fair game.

"Cause," Kayla said, confidently. "Mama did something to me that she just shouldn't have done."

"That's not what she said," Linell said.

Kayla looked into the rearview mirror, her eyes scolding her younger sister. She didn't like the idea that she was basically stepping in to play mother to these children, when their own mother wouldn't, and one of them would go as far as questioning her.

"Well, what I tell you about what Mama says?" Kayla asked, as if the answer was obvious. "Who do you believe? Who has been the one getting you up and ready for school in the morning, huh? Who doin' that for you?"

"You are," both Latrell and Linell said at the same time.

"Exactly," Kayla said. "Half the time, we don't even know where Mama be at. She gon' slap me like I done did something wrong to her, so I slapped her back."

"Oh," Linell said. "Okay."

Kayla was so ready to move on and talk about something else. While she drove the rest of the way back to Lyesha's house over the east side, she felt a little odd that she simply didn't cross Martin Luther King and make her way back to the house on Paris. As the hours and days went on, that house felt less and less like home. Even if they were to ever go back, they just wouldn't feel as comfortable in there. What all went down in the living room was too much to just let go and act as if it had never happened.

Kayla pulled up into the extra space next to Lyesha's garage, just turning in off of the alley.

"Let's go on and get inside," Kayla said to Latrell and Linell. "For all we know, Mama's ass might still be sleep or some shit. I'mma make y'all something to eat." Kayla, herself didn't know what she was going to do with the rest of her time.

This was the time that she would usually be spending with Marcus, especially if he didn't have to go move any weight out in the streets.

Latrell and Linell agreed, the two of them following Kayla into the back door. Inside, Kayla put together an after-school meal for them. She led the two of them into the living room, where they both sat down, their backs against the couch, and watched television. Kayla, feeling relieved that they were settled in, looked at her mother. The woman was just getting up from what looked like a nap, seeing as she was wearing street clothes. There was no telling what she'd gone out and did while Kayla was gone, but Kayla wasn't going to judge her.

Rolanda got up, said hello to everybody, then headed upstairs to use the bathroom. Just as Kayla turned around and was heading back to the kitchen, she heard tires screech outside. Then came what sounded like car doors opening and people stepping out into crunchy snow. Without coming to any conclusions already, Kayla knew exactly what was about to happen. Her heartbeat jumped as she feared the worst and turned around.

"Get down, y'all!" Kayla yelled. "Get down."

No sooner than Kayla had finished her warning, loud booms began to ring in all of their ears. Bullets came flying through the front window, causing Kayla to immediately get down onto the floor, right there in the dining room. Her mind flashed back to the other day, when Marcus' place had been shot up. All she could think about was how scared she was for her life as she got down low in the bathroom. Glass shattered everywhere, spreading out over the carpet like glitter.

A parade of bullets sprayed into Lyesha's house. The three of them screamed and squealed, not knowing where to go or where to hide to get away from the attack. Within a matter of seconds, it was all over after maybe two dozen bullets or so. Once everything got quiet, Kayla felt it was safe enough to stand up. She quickly, but cautiously, walked into the living room. There, she found Latrell, clearly looking as if he'd just been through something horrible. Out of instinct, Kayla hugged Latrell, pulling him extra close to her body.

"I'm so sorry," Kayla said, feeling guilt consume her. "I swear, I'm so sorry."

She then allowed Latrell to step away from her as he headed toward the staircase to meet his mother, Rolanda, who was quickly coming down the steps. "Oh my God!" Rolanda yelled. "You gotta be fuckin' kiddin' me."

Kayla walked ahead, noticing that Linell's foot was sticking out from the side of the couch. Quickly, Kayla jumped over to the couch and found her little sister's body, sprawled out on the floor next to the couch. She fell to the ground and grabbed her body.

"No, no, no," Kayla said, sounding desperate to hear her sister's voice. "Linell! Linell!"

"What?" Roland asked, rushing over. "What happened to her?"

No sooner than Rolanda finished asking that question, she'd seen exactly what happened. Her little girl Linell had been hit by one of the bullets. Instantly, a huge scream came out of Rolanda's mouth – the kind of scream that was piercing to Kayla and Latrell's ears; the kind of scream that told anyone within a couple of blocks that a mother had just seen something horrific happen to her child.

"We gotta get her to a hospital," Rolanda said, frantically. "Kayla! We gotta get her to a hospital."

Seeing that Linell was unresponsive, Rolanda screamed again and shook her body, trying to get her to come to life a little bit. It didn't take Rolanda long to see that the bullet had hit her daughter in the stomach. Blood came gushing out of her body, dying the carpet underneath her red.

Kayla jumped up and grabbed the car keys. She and her mother then picked Linell up, one holding her shoulders and head and the other holding her legs. They quickly carried her out of the house, through the back door, and across the snow-covered backyard. With Latrell closing the door behind them, they all huddled into the car.

"Hurry up, Kayla!" Rolanda said, sitting in the backseat with her child as Kayla got behind the wheel. "We gotta hurry up and get her to a hospital. What would be the closest one?"

Rolanda looked down at Linell, begging and praying that she would start talking at any minute.

"I don't know," Kayla said, her heart really beating. "Probably Methodist... downtown."

"Whatever!" Rolanda yelled. "I don't care. Just hurry up and get my baby to a hospital."

Kayla started the engine and quickly pulled out of the makeshift driveway. She rushed out to Keystone Avenue and headed toward downtown. Whatever stoplights were red on her way, if there weren't any cars coming her way, she would go ahead and cross at the intersection.

` "Drive, Kayla!" Rolanda demanded. "Drive this damn car so we can hurry up and get my baby to a hospital." Rolanda screamed and said a prayer, asking God to please not take her precious child away from her.

Kayla, with tears streaming down her own face, drove as fast as she could as she made her way downtown. She pulled up outside of the Emergency Room at Methodist Hospital. At this point, she was truly in total fear. From what it would seem, Linell could very well be dead. During the ten minutes or so it took them to get to the hospital, the little girl hadn't said a single word to let anyone know that she was still alive. Rolanda cried and cried and cried, cradling her baby in her arms.

When Kayla came to a screeching stop, she quickly jumped out of the car and she and Rolanda carried Linell into the hospital. As soon as they were inside, their entrance having made a huge scene in the Emergency Room, a couple of hospital workers rushed over, asking what had happened.

"She's been shot!" Rolanda yelled, answering their question. "My baby been shot! Please, don't let my baby die! Pleaseee, don't let my baby die."

The hospital staff assured Rolanda that they would do everything they could as they rushed Linell through some double doors on a stretcher. Rolanda, at her daughter's side, told Linell over and over again that the doctors were going to save her. What the little girl could actually hear, known of them knew.

Kayla followed her mother and the stretcher all the way back to the operating room. Here, she and Rolanda were asked to step outside as a team of doctors and nurses came swooshing into the room to do what they do best. They insisted it would be best if the mother and siblings were not in the room to see, or get in the way of whatever was about to happen. Only wanting her daughter to be saved, Rolanda grabbed Latrell and Kayla by the arms, the two of them clearly very distressed, and led them out into the hallway.

The first thing Rolanda did was look into the operating room. She shook her head, rambling to herself, begging God. After a few minutes of doing this, her head turned, almost looking like something in a scary movie. Her eyes were full of rage as she turned and looked at Kayla.

"You little bitch!" Rolanda yelled. "Who the fuck you tell where we was stayin'?"

Kayla immediately began to shake her head. "I ain't tell nobody where we was stayin'," she answered. "I swear I didn't, Mama."

Rolanda moved closer, not liking her daughter's response. She yelled. "Well, you must'a done told somebody, Kayla," she said. "I mean, how the fuck else would they just so happen to come shootin' up the house where you stayin'. It's probably them same damn crazy ass niggas. Oh my God, you done let the fools find out where we stayin' again, and all over that nigga, Marcus."

Kayla was genuinely confused – confusion that would blind her and make her totally miss just how enraged her mother was becoming. Right then and there, Rolanda reached out and slapped Kayla as hard as she could. Curse words slipped through the woman's lips as she quickly moved in on her daughter, ready to beat her ass.

"Mama, I swear!" Kayla said, pleading. "I ain't tell nobody where we was stayin'."

Rolanda swung on her daughter as if she was in a full-blown fist fight out on the street with some chick who'd said the wrong thing to her today. Rolanda was so filled with rage that she just couldn't control herself. She swung on Kayla like there was no tomorrow, causing Kayla to push back in self-defense. Kayla, who was now crying herself, couldn't help but feel angry and guilty. If Linell died in that operating room, there was no way that her mother would ever forgive her. In so many ways, Kayla blamed herself for even being in this mess. Beyond that, she blamed Marcus; he was able to go stay out of town while her life had basically transformed into a living hell.

Soon enough, hospital security guards were pulling Rolanda off of Kayla. "I hate you!" Rolanda yelled, tears running down her cheeks. "I fuckin' hate you, bitch! I hate you! You done got my little girl killed!" She looked at the security guards, calmed herself down, and told them to let her go. After a few seconds, they did just that.

Rolanda pointed at Kayla. "You little bitch!" she said. "I swear to God, I don't even wanna see you again in life. You done told somebody where we was stayin' and now gon' lie to my face like I don't even know it. How else would they come shootin' up Lyesha's house, huh? How else would they know we was there?"

Kayla, at a loss for words, could only look at her mother and shake her head. She knew that she hadn't told anyone, but the events of the day were certainly saying otherwise. Before Kayla could even come up with a response, Rolanda turned and marched away. She mumbled something as Kayla watched her back walk away from her. Ashamed, Kayla could only look into the eyes of the hospital security, who all looked at her with questioning eyes. Deep in her feelings, she turned away and pushed back through the double doors, through the Emergency Room lobby, and out to her car. She got behind the wheel and drove off, not really knowing where she was going. This left little Latrell, standing there in the hallway in complete silence and astonishment.

Kayla drove around the hospital before pulling over on Capital Street, on the other side of the complex. She broke down and cried, turning the radio down. She looked out at the people walking by her on the street, having no idea what she was going through. Kayla leaned her head back against the seat and asked God, "Why Linell, God? Why?"

Kayla eventually parked the car inside of the hospital parking garage. Just outside of the hospital, between the hospital building and the parking garage, was a little courtyard. Sure, it was covered in snow, but for once the cold weather had done Kayla a favor. It would give her some privacy as nobody else would be in the little park setting.

Kayla walked out into the courtyard, hardly being able to wipe all of the tears away from her face. When she cleared a little area of snow on a bench to sit down, she immediately pulled out her phone. Sniffling, she called Marcus, hoping that he would answer. She didn't have a particular reason for calling him. It just felt like the right thing to do at that moment.

"Hello?" Marcus answered, clearly sounding as if he'd been relaxing.

Just as Kayla was about to force his name out of her mouth, she broke down into tears. She sobbed. Right away, Marcus tuned in to her cries, knowing that something bad had happened.

"What's wrong, Kayla?" Marcus asked. "What's wrong, baby?"

Kayla pulled herself together enough to explain. "It's Linell," she said. "They came by where we was stayin' today, Marcus. They came by there."

"They what?" Marcus asked. "What you talkin' about, Kayla?"

"Them niggas came over to my Godmother Lyesha's house, Marcus," Kayla explained. "That's where we was stayin'. They came over there like thirty minutes ago and," she took a break to cry really hard, "they shot into the house, right when we had just got there from me picking them up from school. And they hit Linell."

"Fuck," Marcus said, that being one of the last things in the world he ever wanted to hear. "Is she gon' be okay, Kayla? Did y'all get her to a hospital? What they say when y'all got there?"

"I don't know," Kayla said, answering Marcus' first question. "And yeah, we got her to a hospital. They are operating on her right now. I'm sittin' out in a courtyard kinda thing while I talk to you, until I go back in there. God, please don't let Linell die. Please!"

"What you doin' out in the courtyard?" Marcus asked, wondering why she wasn't inside and waiting on the doctors to come out of the operating room.

"Out in the hallway," Kayla said. "When me and my mama and Latrell were basically shuffled out of the room and into the hallway, Mama started blaming me for all this. She thinks it's all my fault, Marcus. Oh my God, if Linell dies, my mama gon' blame me forever."

"It's not your fault, it's not your fault," Marcus said, feeling much of the blame himself. "Man, I swear. I'mma kill that nigga Hakim. He takin' this shit too far. I'mma be back down there tonight. Just wait till my cousin come walkin' through the door."

"What you talkin' about, Marcus?" Kayla asked. "Your cousin ain't gon just get in the car and drive you back down to Indianapolis like that."

"I ain't say he had to do shit for me," Marcus said. "I'mma drive myself."

Marcus told Kayla about how he was going to do whatever he needed to do to get back down to Indianapolis. All Kayla could do was cry, realizing that she needed to get back in the building and see what the doctors were saying about Linell. However, now things felt personal. Now even Kayla felt a little rage boiling in her blood for Hakim, and she'd never met the dude. If Linell died, she would literally become Hakim's worst nightmare. She was very sure of that.

Kayla ended the call with Marcus, telling him that she would call him back later on and fill him in on what was going on. Marcus promised that, one way or another, he was going to ride down from Fort Wayne. Kayla, not being able to take anything he said seriously, hung up the phone. She made her way back into the hospital and zigzagged through the long hallways until she came back to the Emergency Room area. She walked up to Latrell, knowing that she really didn't need to be in her mother's face at the moment.

"What did Mama say so far?" Kayla asked Latrell. "Has she come out and said anything?"

It was very clear to Kayla that her little brother was having a hard time dealing with his sister being shot. Even though they did bicker and fight with one another, he really did love his little sister deep down in his heart. In so many ways, it was as if they were the best of friends really.

Latrell shook his head. "No," he said. "I ain't even seen her."

Just as Latrell said this to Kayla, Rolanda came walking around the bend in the hallway. She stepped up to the window, watching how the nurses and doctors huddled around Linell's bed. Even though she was mad beyond belief at Kayla for even pulling her family into this horrible mess, she still, as any mother would, could only focus on her child's life. Minutes later, a man who was clearly the doctor came walking out. He was tall and white, with thick black glasses. Rolanda looked up at the man and started crying. He quickly grabbed the woman and told her that her daughter was going to be okay, but there may have been some serious damage to her organs.

Kayla, seeing that her mother was clearly going through something, pulled herself together and walked down the hallway. Rolanda looked at her daughter then back to the doctor. "So, she is gonna be all right, though, right?" she asked. "She is going to live, right?"

The doctor nodded. "Yes, Miss. Yes, she will," he answered.

Rolanda was relieved to hear that. "What kind of damage might there be?" she then asked the doctor.

"We don't really know yet," he answered. "We've stopped the bleeding and she's been stabilized, for now. If everything goes okay, I'll be able to tell you that we're out of the woods, so to speak, and then we can explore the range of damage you might expect as a result of a child her age and size suffering a bullet wound. The bullet, Miss, punctured her kidney, which isn't the worst possible scenario, but it certainly isn't the best. We're preparing her for surgery now."

Kayla hyperventilated, her nostrils flaring as the anger built inside of her. "I'mma kill this nigga," Kayla said. "I'mma kill this nigga myself and be done with all of this."

Without even so much as saying two words to her mother, Kayla turned around and walked straight out of the hospital. Back outside, now facing 16th Street, Kayla pulled her phone out of her pocket and texted Marcus, asking for Roy's number. When Marcus responded asking why, Kayla simply told him that she needed his number and she needed it right away. With no further argument, Marcus sent Roy's number to Kayla and Kayla called Roy. She was ready, now more than ever, to do something about this problem.

Chapter 10

The first thing Hakim did when he woke up that day, around noon, was go down to the basement and check on his guest, Lorna. He had practically woken up with a smile on his face. What were the fucking chances that he would get the nigga's mother? Now, Hakim knew that all he had to do was wait. *Just give the nigga a little time*, Hakim thought to himself last night. *When the little nigga sees that his mama done gone missing, he will come right out and I'mma get his ass. All I gotta do is wait and he will come poppin' up.*

Hakim had a few errands to run, having felt a little funny that he didn't wake up to Amber sucking his dick like he normally might. Last night, he had talked her into going to stay with one of her sisters over on the south side while he finished up with some business. He was planning on all of this to be over in just a couple of days. He had the nigga's mama, downstairs in a spare bedroom, naked. And Raul and Jayrone had shot up wherever the girlfriend went back to. These two things combined were enough to surely fire Marcus up and get him to do something stupid.

When Hakim got back from the house with a few shopping bags, he sat them down onto his dining room table and headed back down to the basement. At some point during the night, he could hear Lorna trying to get out. He'd had company over, the kind who knew exactly what kind of man Hakim was out in the streets. If anyone had a single question about anything, they knew better than to ask. If they'd heard anything in Hakim's house, coming from the basement, they would just keep it to themselves and act as if nothing was happening. It was just as simple as that.

Upon getting to the landing, and looking out across his finished basement and toward the door, he was a bit amazed that the woman hadn't tried to break through the door. Everything looked to be in the same place it had been when he'd come down to give her a little something to eat for breakfast. Hakim opened the door and looked at Lorna's thick body on the bed.

"You all right?" he asked her, sounding very soothing in the quiet house.

Lorna looked at Hakim with hate-filled eyes. "Fuck you!" she said. "Fuck you nigga."

"Remember what happened last night when you went beggin' for the dick," Hakim said. "I gave it to you. Don't act like you didn't like this shit." He motioned toward his manhood. "Every woman I break off with a little bit of this dick... They always come back wanting more. And I see you still here."

Lorna remained silent. Hakim chuckled, stepping out of the room to grab a knife. Curse words slipped out of Lorna's mouth when he came walking back into the room. Hakim sat on the edge of the bed, reaching for Lorna's thick thighs.

"I don't know why you gotta make this hard, baby," Hakim said. "Just tell me where the little nigga is and everybody's life is gon' be easier. The longer y'all wait, the more fucked up shit is gonna get. Little Kayla doing a whole lot worse than you right now."

Lorna's eyes opened wide. "Kayla?" she said. "Nigga, you betta not hurt that girl anymore. Don't do shit to her, nigga. She ain't got nothin' to do with this!"

Hakim laughed. "I didn't say I was going to hurt her," he said. "Just might scare her a little bit, is all. And we gon' keep scarin' people, all around this city until Marcus turn up somewhere...until y'all niggas get the point."

Lorna's head shook. More than anything, she just wanted to be out of this room. She still hadn't managed to figure out exactly where she was. What part of the city?

"Don't shake your head," Hakim said, smiling. "And we gon' get that brother of yours, too. All we gotta do is wait," he said, reaching out toward her calves. "All we gotta do is wait. But, in the meantime, why don't you give a nigga some of that pussy, so he don't get bored while we waitin'."

Hakim stood up and slammed the door shut. When he turned around, he dropped his pants and stepped out of them. He then slid his shirt up over his hand. Lorna backed away, toward the headboard of the bed. As soon as Hakim was lowering himself onto her pleasantly thick body, she kicked and screamed. Quickly, Hakim put the knife to her throat, causing Lorna to go silent immediately and stop kicking. "Don't kill me," Lorna pleaded. "Please, you ain't gotta do all this. I swear... You ain't gotta do all this."

"Bitch, keep fuckin' round," Hakim said, warning her, "and that nigga is gon' find his mama dead in a minute, watch out." He pushed her legs open. "This ain't gon' hurt, I promise. It never does."

Lorna calmed down, opening her legs as she was told. "Why are you doin' this?" she asked, tears rolling down her face. "Why are you doing this?"

"Bitch, shut up," Hakim told her, holding the knife at her throat. He leaned in and pushed himself inside of her. Never had Lorna felt so disgusted in her life. And it certainly had been a long time since she had let some man she'd just met penetrate her without protection. It all felt so nasty, and Hakim's deep voice only made her feel dirtier about it.

Hakim stroked into Lorna in the missionary position, then telling her to turn over. If she tried anything tricky, the knife would be on her throat. Lorna, wanting to stay alive even if only so that her existence would help protect her son Marcus, turned over. Reluctantly, she arched her back. Never had so much fear riveted through her body.

"Damn, you got a big ass," Hakim said, slapping it. He then entered her, holding her hips with his firm grip. After stroking for several minutes, putting a lot of force into his thrusts, he released inside of Lorna. As soon as he pulled out, Lorna moved further up onto the bed and turned around, her arms now hugging her chest. She looked at Hakim with eyes that were full of spit. She had wished she'd had something that would kill this nigga and she could do it herself. He was a monster, by any definition of the word.

Hakim backed away from the bed and slowly slid back into his clothes. "You a feisty little bitch," he said. "A little older than I normally go for a bitch, but you still go the body I like. I will say that. A lot of these younger chicks out here ain't even as thick as you are."

"Go to hell," Lorna told him, wiping her back against the comforter to get some of his sweat off of her.

Hakim chuckled, just as he was finishing up with putting his shirt on. "I don't know about you," he said. "A nigga might have to keep you here even when I do find the nigga."

"You not gon' find him, nigga," Lorna said. "You not gon' find him."

Hakim, never liking when a woman talked so disrespectfully to a man, quickly stepped forward. With the palm of his hand wide open, he wrapped his fingers around Lorna's neck, holding her in place. She gagged and coughed, reminding Hakim of the way some women would react when he pushed himself into their throats. He chuckled just thinking of that.

"Don't tell me what I will and won't do," Hakim said, talking very quietly and looking dead into Lorna's eyes. "Like I told you, one way or another, we gon' find that nigga. I know he alive and we gon' find his ass. He stole some of my shit and fucked my chick. Oh yeah." He nodded up and down, smiling. "The moment he put his dick in what belonged to me, the nigga was basically hanging himself. Only a matter of time at this point...only a matter of time."

Hakim tightened his grip around Lorna's neck for the last couple of seconds before backing away from her. He got a real kick out of the power he had over her, watching her barely move while she had been in his grip. He slapped her thighs before leaving the room and shutting the door, locking it behind him.

"I gotta go make this money," he said to her, through the door. "I'll be back to see you in a little bit."

When Hakim left the room, Lorna couldn't do anything but hug herself as tight as possible. Never in her life had she been violated, and so roughly. The very thought of having to stay in this room, wherever she was, made her sick. No clothes. No phone. No computer. She was literally a prisoner, and in many ways, something for Hakim, and whoever it was that brought her into this place yesterday, to use whenever they wanted to.

All alone in this room, she laid down onto the bed and pulled a sheet up over her body. She wanted to reach out to somebody, anybody, and let them know where she was. However, she too knew that it would only be a matter of time – a matter of time before Roy and Marcus noticed that she wasn't at home; that she wasn't answering her phone. She could only hope that whatever actions they took would be enough to meet with Hakim's. In the flesh, he seemed to be ten times as scary as he did when she was just hearing about him.

***

Roy was laying up with Cherry today. A lot was on his mind. Brandon and Juan were due to be coming over at a moment's notice so they could roll up on Hakim over at his house on Cold Springs Road. Even if he wasn't at that particular house, the fact that they were there and were bold enough to run up in there would send a message to Hakim if nothing else: They were not fucking around with him when it came to Marcus.

Roy could hear his phone vibrating from his pocket in his pants on the floor. Feeling somewhat lazy, he reached down to answer it. Just as he was about to answer, Cherry rose up onto her elbows and began to play with his soft manhood. He smiled as he spoke into the phone.

"Wassup?" Roy answered the phone.

"Roy?" the female voice said. "Is this Roy? Roy?"

It was obvious to Roy that whoever this chick was had been worked up. Immediately, he pushed Cherry's head away and tried to figure out who he was talking to.

"Yeah, yeah," he said, sounding concerned. "Who the fuck is this?"

"This is Kayla," she said. "Marcus's girlfriend."

"Kayla?" Roy asked. "Oh, hey wassup, baby? How you doin'?"

"Not good," Kayla said. "Not good. I wanna kill this nigga myself."

Surprised to hear Kayla using that kind of language, Roy immediately knew right away that something major was up. "What you talkin' bout, Kayla? What you talkin' about?"

"That nigga, Hakim," Kayla said. "He shot up where me and my family was hidin', Roy. He shot the shit up and got my little sister, Linell. She only nine years old." Kayla sobbed briefly before pulling it back together. "One of the bullets got her, in her stomach. We at the hospital now, Methodist, downtown."

Roy took a deep breath. He didn't like what he was hearing the least bit. Hearing this only pushed him more into the idea of putting a bullet into Hakim's head. Then, and only then, none of them would have to worry about stuff like this happening again. It was becoming very evident that there was no other option.

"Calm down, Kayla," Roy said. "Calm down. Did she make it or what?" He hated having to ask that kind of question, especially about a small child who would never deserve to be shot for anything.

"Yeah," Kayla said, "but right before I left, the doctor was sayin' somethin' to my mama bout how there might be damage and stuff. They operatin' on her now, so we'll know when he get done. God, I hope she pull through okay. Please don't let this hurt my sister for the rest of her life. Please."

Roy nodded, his nostrils flaring up. "I see, I see," he said.

"I know you got somethin' planned, Roy," Kayla said. "I just know you do. This nigga –this monster – gotta be stopped. Roy, he is takin' this shit tooooo far! Tooooo far! God, we gotta kill his ass before he get us. We got to. I don't even know how he found out where I was stayin' or anything. I swear, I ain't tell nobody…not one person. My mama thinks I did and now she blame me."

Roy's head shook at Cherry, as she herself was seeing that whoever was on the other end was talking about something very serious. "When can you come by the house?" Roy asked, knowing that the sooner they could jump into action, the better. There was no tellin' what Hakim was going to do, and there was no telling who he had helping him. He seemed to know a lot of things without someone specifically telling him.

"Kayla, Kayla, calm down," Roy said, trying to get her to simply talk to where he could understand. "When can you come through the house? You remember where I stay? We gon' get this nigga, even if it's the last thing we do."

Just as Roy was waiting on Kayla to respond, he heard a beep in his ear. There was another person calling, on the other line. He pulled the phone away from his face and saw that it was Marcus.

Chapter 11

When Marcus hung up with Kayla, he couldn't help but feel like the pit of his stomach was dropping out of him. He felt not only sorry, but guilty. The truth of the matter is, no matter how he looked at this situation, it all started with him. Sure, he knew he didn't take the part of the missing brick. However, at the same time, smashing Tweety on Hakim's back porch was probably not the best decision. Never did he think any of his actions would wind up causing Kayla so much trouble.

Marcus paced around his cousin Larry's apartment for a minute, knowing that he'd be coming home within a matter of minutes. He called his mother, for the third time today. No answer.

Looking down at his phone screen, Marcus scrolled back through his text messages. He'd even sent his mother a text message a few times and she hadn't responded. Even with her being at work, it wasn't like her to not respond at all, especially if she saw that it was her child trying to get into contact with her. Frustrated and confused, Marcus began to get a feeling. His palms became sweaty; his heart thumped a little harder than usual.

"Why Mama ain't answerin'?" Marcus said out loud. At this point, he couldn't deny any longer the feeling in his soul – in the pit of his stomach. Something just wasn't right. He needed to have somebody go check on his mama and see why she wasn't answering her phone.

Marcus called his uncle Roy.

"Hello, Marcus?" Roy answered, clearly sounding a little more worked up than he would normally be.

"Yeah, Uncle, this me," Marcus said. "We got a problem."

"I know we do, nigga," Roy said. "I just got off the phone with Kayla, on the other line."

"I know," Marcus said, cutting his uncle's sentence off. "I know. She just called and told me. About her little sister gettin' shot. I can't believe this shit, Uncle. I can't believe this shit."

"Yeah, that's what she was tellin' me," Roy said. "It look like that nigga Hakim gettin' a little more aggressive. When I went and met with him, I could see it in his eyes. We gon' have to kill this nigga or else he gon' kill us."

"Just what I was thinkin'," Marcus said, nodding his head. "That's just what I was thinkin'. But I was callin' to ask you, Uncle, if you had talked to my mama today. You talked to her?"

"Naw," Roy said. "I ain't talked to her yet today. I was over her house last night or whenever. I had to help her clear some space out in the garage so that she could put your car in there. She just had the thing sitting out in the driveway. I told her straight from the jump when I got there that that shit just wasn't gon' work. She needed to hide the car."

"I'm try'na get back down to Indianapolis," Marcus said. "I been callin' Mama all day and she ain't answered. I got a bad feeling, Uncle – a bad feeling."

"Maybe she at work or something, Marcus," Roy suggested.

"Naw," Marcus said, shaking his head. "Even if she at work, she at least answer her texts even if she can't call me back right away. I'm tellin' you, man. I done called her a couple of times, and I done been hitting her up through text. She ain't responded to none of them. Her job don't be havin' her that busy to the point where she can't even answer a text. Just roll over to her place and make sure she alright. I just got a bad feeling."

Roy understood where his nephew was coming from, and there was nothing wrong with him wanting someone to check on his mother. In a time like this, anyone could not be answering their phone for the worst of reasons. "Hold up, though," Roy said. "Nigga, how are you gon' get back down to Indianapolis? I told your girl to come through in a little bit. She talkin' like she gon' kill Hakim her damn self. I can't believe that nigga went after her family again and done shot the little girl. That's just some coldhearted shit."

"Yeah, that is," Marcus said. "And, fuck, I don't know. I'mma hitchhike back down there if I got to. I can't just sit up here doin' nothin' while Kayla and her family having to run and hide and dodge bullets. I'mma grown man. I'm comin' back down to Indianapolis. I don't give a fuck what y'all say."

Marcus talked to his uncle for a few minutes more, listening to how he had talked to Brandon and Juan about Hakim, as well as some more details about their meeting. Roy even went as far as talking about some of the ideas he had shared with Brandon and Juan about running up in Hakim's house and killing any and everyone inside.

As Roy was deep in conversation, Marcus noticed that he heard the apartment door opening downstairs. Within a matter of seconds, footsteps were climbing the steps. Keys jingled. Marcus told his uncle that he'd have to call him back when he had a plan because Larry was coming home from work. Since the last thing Roy needed right now was for his sister to know that he'd been talking to her son, he was quick to end the conversation. Roy simply promised Marcus that he would ride over to Lorna's house and make sure that everything was okay.

Larry opened the door, carrying his gray bag at his side. He lifted the bag up over his head before dropping it onto the couch.

"Wassup cus?" Larry asked.

Marcus nodded. "Wassup?" he said. "You just now gettin' off of work?" Marcus, unsure how Larry might react to taking him back down to Indianapolis, decided to tread lightly with the conversation.

"Yeah," Larry said, nodding his head. "Bout to take a shower and shit."

Marcus noticed how he'd sat his keys down on the counter in his kitchenette.

"You wanna go out and get something to eat when I get a shower in and change clothes?" Larry asked.

Marcus shrugged, feeling the pain in his shoulder as he'd forgotten that shrugging probably wasn't the best thing for him to be doing. "Sure, it's whatever," he answered.

Larry said that wherever Marcus wanted to eat was fine and for him to just let him get his shower in and he'd be ready to go. Soon enough, Larry had disappeared back to his bedroom. Next thing Marcus knew, he could hear the shower going. For a few minutes, he gave some real thought to propositioning Larry to take him back down to Indianapolis. However, after some thinking, Marcus knew that doing this just wouldn't work. Larry had always been the good one in the family – the one who went to church almost every Sunday and sometimes on Wednesday nights. There was no way, knowing how close he was to Lorna, that Larry would agree to taking Marcus back down into the firestorm that was Hakim looking for him. However, Marcus knew that he had to do something. Desperate times really did call for desperate measures.

Marcus' eyes zeroed in on Larry's keys sitting on the kitchen counter. He knew it would be wrong to take his cousin's car; however, what other choice did he have? It was obvious that Hakim was going to kill everyone to get to Marcus. This helped Marcus to realize that he needed to jump into action before anyone that he truly cared about took a bullet that wasn't really meant for them. Sitting like a duck, two hours north of Indianapolis just wasn't going to cut it.

Marcus struggled with sliding into his coat. Once he was in it, however, with his fixed up arm underneath one side, he grabbed Larry's keys and headed out of the door, closing it very softly behind him. He climbed into Larry's car, constantly keeping his eyes on Larry's windows up above. If he was going to steal his cousin's car, he at least didn't want the dude to have to come running out in his bath towel to try to stop it from happening. Once Marcus flipped the clearly economically-budgeted car into DRIVE, he backed out of the parking spot and headed out toward the main road. He turned left, somewhat retracing the way his mother had taken to get him to Larry's apartment. After getting turned around a little bit in Downtown Fort Wayne, Marcus managed to find the very same street that he remembered led out to the city's west side so that he could get onto I-69. Once the highway ramp was in sight, he called his uncle Roy, who was heading out the door himself. "I'm on my way," he said. "I'll be there in about two hours or somethin' like that."

With so much rage and frustration, Marcus managed to control Larry's car by just using one arm. He quickly headed south. The built-up urban areas that comprised Fort Wayne were increasingly further behind him, fading in the distance. He put the pedal to the metal and drove toward Indianapolis. It was so hard for him to not go all of 100 miles an hour.

***

When Roy had hung up the phone with Marcus, he was getting into his car. He, too, had just called Lorna. And like Marcus had said to him just minutes before, there was no answer. As Roy headed over to the east side to his sister's house, he really thought that Lorna was either busy at work or was at home taking a nap. He knew that his sister could handle herself, and he didn't think that anyone had figured out where Marcus' mother lived.

When Roy turned at the stop sign at the end of Lorna's block and began to roll closer to her house, he could already feel that something was very wrong. The house, even from a distance, looked desolate. Lorna's car was in the driveway, which was a good sign. However, Roy tried to figure out if this bad feeling of his was really paranoia or his gut, trying to tell him that something bad had happened to his sister.

Roy pulled up out front. As soon as he stepped out of the car and headed up the driveway, he noticed how the tracks that Lorna's car made in the snow on the first part of the driveway – the part that was between the sidewalk and the street – looked to have gotten a light cover up of snow. This was odd to Roy, especially since he didn't know that it had snowed much at all during the day. The wind could have very well blown snow over the tracks. However, the tracks would surely look a lot fresher than that if Lorna had been out today.

Roy walked up to the door and knocked, yelling Lorna's name. There was no response. He stood there, quietly, trying to listen to see if he could hear her moving or anything on the inside. Once again, there was nothing. Roy began to feel that something was going on. He walked around to the back of the house, his heart thumping when he saw that his sister's back door was just standing open. This was something that she would never, in a million years, do.

Without even thinking, Roy pulled his gun out of his inside coat pocket. He stepped into her kitchen and looked around. There was a pot on the stove and a cup on the table, letting Roy know that the last thing Lorna had done in here was start to make some tea. Cautiously, Roy moved forward through the house. First, he checked the living room and the dining room. There was no one there. He then checked the basement. As usual, it looked like a big catch-all room. When Roy saw the three bedrooms and two bathrooms, he thought he understood what had happened. There were several bullet holes in the master bedroom wall, directly from where the door opened. He knew right away that Lorna had shot from the room across the hall at whomever had come after her. However, with her not being here, these mystery people must have either had backup or have been able to get her out of her own house in some way.

Roy put his gun down at his side and drove his fists into his thighs. "Fuck!" he said, very angrily. "I'mma kill that nigga." Roy rushed back toward the back door, pulling it closed. "I'mma kill that nigga," he said again. "He got my sister. I'mma kill that nigga."

Roy walked back around the side of the house and got into his car. When he pulled up to the stop sign at the corner, beginning to turn, he called Brandon and Juan and told them that their asses had better be at his house as soon as fucking possible. Hakim was terrorizing Marcus's girlfriend, Kayla, and her family. And he had apparently taken Marcus' mother as a hostage, leaving Roy to wonder how Hakim had even found out where Lorna lived. Confused and starting to taste a little blood in his mouth, Roy headed back over to the west side in thought.

"This nigga Hakim know just what he doin'," Roy said to himself at a stoplight not too far from Lorna's house. "He try'na do the shit that he know is gon' bring Marcus out of hiding." He thought about how his nephew was just so determined to get back down to Indianapolis, and was on his way at this point.

"A'ight then," Roy said. "He wanna draw a little attention to his self, that's exactly what he gon' get."

Earlier, Roy had been thinking about whether or not it was necessary to run up into Hakim's house and just kill everybody. At this point, he couldn't even really care. Whoever got killed wouldn't cause him to lose any sleep at night. Furthermore, it was looking like it was necessary, even if only on the principle of *it's better you than me*.

When Roy got home, he marched right into his house. Cherry came from around the hallway wall, looking at him as he had just walked through the front door. She was prepared to be his little freak for him. However, upon seeing his face, it was obvious to her that he probably wouldn't be in the mood for all of that.

"What's wrong?" Cherry asked, coming over toward Roy.

Roy shook his head as he was pulling his gun out of his coat and setting it down onto the coffee table in his living room. "That nigga got my sister," he told Cherry. "I just came from over my sister house because Marcus was sayin' that she ain't been answerin' her phone all damn day. I went over there to see what was up. Her fuckin' back door is kicked in and there were bullet holes in her bedroom wall."

"No," Cherry said, covering her mouth. "You not serious."

"I am, Cherry," Roy said. "I am fuckin' serious. Tonight," Roy was clearly about business, "We all gon' have to roll up in that nigga's house and kill his ass. He takin' this shit a little too far."

Cherry thought about the call Roy had received from Kayla just minutes before he left the house. Even to her, it definitely sounded like this Hakim person was vicious and would stop at nothing.

"Get the house ready, baby," Roy told Cherry. "We gon' be havin' some company in a little bit. Marcus on his way in, Kayla said she'd be over here as soon as she could get here, and I told Brandon and Juan that them little niggas had betta get here as soon as they fuckin' can. Somebody's gonna die tonight."

Roy sat down on the couch, remembering that he need to meet up with his connect about the guns with silencers. With that thought in mind, he pulled his phone out and called.

"Get me something to drink, Cherry," he ordered. "And I don't give a fuck what it is. I just need somethin' to calm my shit down a little bit, you know."

Not wanting to resist the least bit, Cherry turned around and headed to the kitchen. Within a couple of minutes, Roy was on the phone with his gun connect, arranging to head back out of the door to go pick them up. He was so determined that he was willing to pay whatever price. This was going to be a silent party, no matter what, and it was going to be very well planned out.

Cherry came walking into the room, handing a glass of Patron on the rocks to Roy. While Roy would normally sip this drink, he gulped it down, pushing his head back. When he looked back forward, he shook his head. "I'mma kill that nigga," he said, to himself, while imagining Hakim's face. "I'mma kill that nigga, I swear to God I am."

Chapter 12

Roy went and met up with his gun connect, whose name happened to be Melvin. Melvin was an older dude who probably was in his mid to upper fifties. However, he still had an ear to the street. Furthermore, he still had his connections in his hometown of Chicago. That opened up the door for Roy to get even better guns. However, Roy really didn't care about all of that. He just made sure that Melvin knew that he needed guns that would shoot as quiet as mechanically possible. Melvin nodded, smoking his cigar as he handed the guns over and took the money from Roy.

"Damn, nigga," Melvin said, being able to see the anger in Roy's face. "You really try'na go kill a nigga, ain't you?"

"When a nigga mess with my family," Roy said, shaking his head. "I gotta kill'em. Ain't no other choice."

Roy didn't stick around much longer to chit chat with Melvin. Instead, he headed out the door, got into his car, and got back home as quickly as he could. Upon arriving to his house and pulling up, Roy saw that Brandon and Juan were already parked out front. He smiled, liking how Marcus' boys were showing up and coming through for him. That was a good sign, and he'd be sure to let Lorna know. Now, however, it was time to see what they were really capable of and just how far they'd go.

"Wassup, niggas?" Roy asked, greeting both Brandon and Juan. "C'mon so we can get inside," he added. "We got some shit we gotta do tonight."

Brandon and Juan looked at one another then followed Roy inside. They both were carrying the heat they'd bought from their connection over on east Washington Street, even though they knew that Roy was coming with something better and something quieter. Once inside, Roy pulled the guns out of a duffle bag and set them both down onto the coffee table. Telling Cherry to go get them some drinks, Roy went ahead and started to talk about the guns.

"Got these from my nigga, Melvin," Roy said. He smiled and held the sleek, titanium guns up. "This shit is nice, ain't it?"

Roy handed one gun to Brandon and the other to Juan. The two of them, standing just inside of the front door were impressed with the guns. They were indeed nice – streamlined, comfortable weight. In addition to that, Brandon and Juan were pretty impressed about seeing the silencers on both guns. They'd never used a gun that had a silencer on it.

"This shit gon' be real quiet, huh?" Juan asked, smiling. He pointed the gun at the wall, pretending to be a rapper or somebody that you would see on TV. "Like how quiet?"

"Ping," was all that Roy said. "All you're going to hear is a ping when you shoot. Then, depending on what you're aiming at, you might here the bullet slamming into a wall or a window shattering. Whatever you hear, it for damn sure won't be no loud boom like you would hear with any other gun."

Brandon began to feel a little nervous. He then realized that everything was quickly seeming kind of rushed. "So, when we runnin' up in there?" he asked. "And we just gon' get buck wild with them like we in some movie or somethin'?"

Roy looked at him, dead into his eyes. "Tonight," he answered. "As soon as it get real good and dark, and there ain't much traffic out on the streets, we gon' run up in there. We got to. He got my sister."

"Your sister?" Juan asked. "Miss Lorna?"

Roy nodded, taking the guns back from them. "Yep," he said. "I rolled over there earlier and she was gone. Saw some bullet holes in the wall and shit. Her back door was hanging wide open. That nigga got my sister and went after Kayla again."

"Went after Kayla again?" Brandon asked, surprised. "What happened this time?"

"Talked to her earlier," Roy said. "And she was tellin' me that when she got back to her mama's friend's house from picking up her little brother and sister from school, bullets started flying through the windows and shit. She called me from the hospital, sounding fucked up and shit."

"Kayla got hit?" Juan asked.

"Naw," Roy answered, shaking his head. "Her little sister, Linell. When I was talkin' to her, she was waiting outside of the hospital and had said that the little girl had been shot and that they was waitin' on the doctors to get done operatin' on her. Hakim is ruthless and the nigga done gone too far. I don't care what Marcus did. Fuck that shit."

Both Brandon and Juan shook their head, their eyes noticing Cherry's curves as she stepped into the room and handed all three men something to drink.

"Tonight," Roy said, making it clear that Brandon and Juan needed to listen to him closely, "we gon' have to be real smart about how we do this shit. Like I already told y'all niggas, Hakim is prolly one of the most prepared niggas in this damn city. Just because we surprisin' him, don't mean that he ain't gon be ready for us. All we gotta do is make sure that we shoot whoever get in our way... And make sure that you shoot to kill. We don't need nobody talkin' after what we doin' tonight, understand?"

Brandon and Juan both swallowed, understanding what they would have to do and nodding their heads. Just then, Roy stepped up to the window and looked out.

"Marcus is pullin' up," he announced. "And some otha car that I don't know. Maybe it's Kayla."

"Kayla?" Juan asked. "What she doin' here if her little sister is in the hospital with a bullet inside of her?"

Roy looked back at the two of them, allowing the blinds to close. "Hakim fuckin' with her family now, and doin' whatever he can to make Kayla's life a living hell. When I was on the phone, I could hear how mad she was. I can tell you this right now, she is ready to kill a nigga, best believe that shit."

***

When Marcus pulled up outside of his Uncle Roy's house, he almost wanted to burst into laughter. Not only had he stolen his cousin Larry's car, but he had also driven the two hours and some change from Fort Wayne – all with only using his one good arm. However, what really made his day was when he saw the car that Kayla drove pulling up out in front of Roy's house at just about the same time as she was pulling up.

Kayla smiled as soon as she made eye contact with Marcus. It was a forced smile, as Linell was still in the hospital and hooked up to all sorts of machines, of which Kayla couldn't even remember the name. When she got out of her car, she and Marcus met between the two on the sidewalk. They hugged, embracing one another with passion. Marcus, sensing that Kayla's nerves truly were on edge, leaned down as he hugged her and kissed her on the side of her head. She smiled, always loving the way Marcus would do that to help her feel better.

"You okay, baby?" Marcus asked Kayla.

Kayla nodded. "I'm try'na be," she answered. "I'm try'na be."

Once they broke apart from one another, Kayla looked up at Marcus. "I didn't know you was here," she said. "And whose car is you drivin'?"

Marcus snickered and looked back at Larry's car. "That's my cousin car," he answered. "The nigga work in real estate or some shit, so this is the car he drive and shit. It's cool, I guess."

"He let you use it?" Kayla asked.

Marcus shook his head, not really wanting to answer. "Naw," he said, reluctantly. "See, what had happened was, well, I took it. When he got in the shower, I snatched his keys off the counter and went out and got in it. I drove all the way down here with just one arm."

Kayla shook her head and playfully slapped Marcus on his good shoulder. "I just hope that Linell makes it through okay," she said. "When I was leaving the hospital, the doctors had just finished up with operating on her and shit, trying to not only get the bullet out but also do something with her kidney or something. That's where the bullet hit her."

"I'm so sorry about this shit," Marcus pleaded, hugging Kayla again. "I swear, Kayla, I ain't mean for none of this to happen."

"Yeah, well," Kayla said, not really knowing what she could even say. "Ain't nothin' we can do about it now, for real, though. I'm down for whatever, though. I'm with your uncle now. We gotta do whatever we gotta do to kill this nigga Hakim before he come after us and kill us all. I don't even know this dude and I'm already gettin' the feelin' that that is the kinda shit he would do."

Marcus shook his head, never having thought it would come to this. "I see my boys is here," he said, pointing at Juan's car, which was parked a couple of spaces down. "That's a good sign."

Marcus and Kayla decided to head inside. As soon as they stepped up to the door, it opened. Roy told them to hurry up and get inside. They did just that, closing the door behind them. When Marcus turned around, his eyes met with Brandon and Juan. Instantly, the two of them jumped up, shook Marcus' hand and hugged him. This was the first time either had seen him since they saw him in the hospital.

"Damn, nigga," Brandon said. "You went ghost on your niggas."

"Yeah," Juan said. "What the fuck is up with that?"

"Had to come back outta hiding," Marcus said. "This nigga done really fucked up. He went after my girl again and got at her family."

"Yeah, that's what your uncle was saying," Juan said. He then looked at Kayla. "Sorry about that," he said. "I hope she pull through okay and be okay and shit."

"And now the nigga done got your mama," Brandon said, without thinking.

Instantly, Marcus' heart sunk and his face bunched up. "Got my mama?" he asked, looking at his uncle Roy.

Roy turned around, not wanting to be the bearer of bad news. "When we got off the phone earlier and shit, Marcus," he said, "I went over to your mama's house." His head shook. "She wasn't there. All I saw was some bullet holes in the wall and her back door was kicked in. From the looks of it, your mama hadn't even moved her car today."

Marcus shook his head and sat down on the couch. Coming to his side to comfort him, Kayla sat down as close as possible to him, telling him that everything was going to be okay.

"Are you serious?" Kayla asked Roy. "This Hakim person really went over there and got Miss Lorna?"

Roy nodded. "That's what it look like to me," he answered. "And we gon' go put a stop to this as soon as it get good and dark outside." Roy lifted the guns he'd gotten up, noticing how Kayla and Marcus looked at each of them. "This shit got silencers on them. We gon' make this shit as quiet as we possibly can, tonight."

Kayla grabbed one gun, then Marcus did. "Man," Marcus said, "if I fire one of these guns off with my good arm, I might mess around and fuck up my other shoulder." Marcus held the gun up, coming to a point where he didn't even care if his other shoulder got messed up. The anger was building inside of him that Hakim had gone as far as to kidnap his mother.

"I thought about that," Roy said, in response. "And that's why I'm thinkin' you just sit and wait on this mission, Marcus."

Marcus jumped up, his chest pumped out. "Sit and wait?" he asked, clearly confused. "I didn't drive all the way down here to just be sittin' around and shit. I could'a did that shit up in Fort Wayne."

"Fort Wayne?" Juan asked, trying to make sense out of what he'd just heard. "What you mean you could'a did that shit up in Fort Wayne? You was up in Fort Wayne, my nigga?"

Marcus took a deep breath, sitting back down. "Yeah," he answered, still feeling a little guilty that he had kept that secret from his boys for the better part of nearly two days. "It was my mama idea," he told them. "She wanted me to go up there until everything smoothed over, whatever that meant. When I talked to my uncle Roy and Kayla and saw that shit was gettin' even worse down here, I stole my cousin's car – that's who I was stayin' with – and headed back down to Naptown. I just got off of the highway and came straight here."

Brandon and Juan glanced at one another. Never would they have thought that Marcus was hiding up in Fort Wayne, and let alone that he wouldn't tell either of them.

"My mama ain't want me to tell nobody," Marcus said, seeing the way Brandon and Juan looked at one another. "I wanted to tell y'all niggas, cause you my boys, and I almost did."

"Naw, you cool," Juan said. "We understand."

Once they all were done talking about Marcus being in Fort Wayne, Roy told Cherry to go relax in the other room while they all talked. He took control of the floor, dominating the conversation.

"Now, what this nigga Hakim is doing is try'na do stuff to draw Marcus out, since he couldn't find him," Roy said. "Don't know how he found out where your mama live, but the nigga knows a lot of people all over the fuckin' city. In fact, I don't even like the five of us sittin' in this house like this. You know it's only a matter of time before he find out where my ass stay and come try'na pull some shit over here. For that matter, don't even be sittin' in front of the window like that. Sit over there." Roy pointed at a couple of chairs, on the other side of the room, where there were no windows against their back. "So, since Hakim is try'na play this game, we gotta play back. When I was leavin' his house, I took a good look at his property and the land around his house. I got some ideas."

Roy sat down and dove right into possible plans. Every so often, somebody would interject with what they thought would work and the group would discuss the idea collectively. Kayla, still nervous and scared for Linell's life, found out that she'd be taking part in this mission as well. Marcus was persistent about being allowed to do something. However, only have one arm made it likely that he would be slowed down. After drawing a little map on a piece of paper to represent what Roy saw of Hakim's house and the land around it, they were better able to make plans for how they would run up in there. Now, Roy knew that he couldn't use the same car he'd used the first time he went to Hakim's. He remembered, though, that there was a vacant property a couple of houses down the street from Hakim. It was then decided that they could use Brandon and Juan's car, since Hakim could very well know what Kayla was driving since he'd managed to get somebody to shoot up where she was staying. They would park at the house down the street and creep up to the property in the dead of the night. Roy could only hope that the plan they'd come up with would work, for the sake of everybody involved.

After making the plans with Marcus, Roy, Juan, and Brandon, Kayla excused herself from the group. She went back out to her car and climbed in behind the wheel. After building up the strength to deal with her mother, she called her.

"Hello?" Rolanda answered, her voice sounding low and filled with anguish.

"Hello, Mama," Kayla said. She didn't really want to talk to her mother any more than her mother wanted to talk to her. "I was just callin' to let you know that if you call me later on tonight, I might not answer."

"Why is that, Kayla?" Rolanda asked. "Why you might not answer your phone if I call?"

"Cause," Kayla said, looking up at the house. "I'm over at Marcus's uncle's house. We gon go after Hakim tonight, the dude that is try'na get Marcus."

"No, no, no," Rolanda said, clearly sounding desperate. "What the fuck you mean you gon' go after Hakim? What are you actually goin' to do? Marcus ain't even here to help with this going after business, so what the fuck you gon' do?"

"He actually is here, Mama," Kayla said. "He inside the house right now. We just talked about everything and all. Marcus drove down from Fort Wayne and just got here."

"Kayla, no," Rolanda said, forgetting how angry she'd been at her daughter just a few hours before in the hospital hallway. "That ain't no good idea. Let them niggas do whatever they gon' do and you do what you gotta do to keep yourself safe. You can't be goin' with them to go after this dude. I mean, damn, girl. You don't even know who the fuck the nigga is or what he look like. Kayla, I don't think this shit is a good idea. I just don't. We'll find somewhere else to go and stuff until they figure all this out. You just get back over here before one of the bullets finally hits you, girl."

"All that don't matter, Mama," Kayla said. "He keep comin' after us. And Linell is lyin' up in the damn hospital with a bullet lodged in her stomach or kidney or whatever. I understand what you sayin', and I appreciate that you really do care about my wellbeing, but I gotta do somethin' to make this stop. First, he had his niggas run up into your house and hold you and us hostage, even pistol whipping you on the side of your head. Then, somehow, because like I said, I ain't tell nobody, not even Marcus, where we was stayin', this Hakim dude managed to find out and come spraying bullets into Lyesha's house. We gotta do something."

Kayla looked back at the house, knowing that it was about time for her to head back inside and see where the conversation, or plans, had gotten to at this point. "Mama, don't worry about me tonight, okay?" Kayla pleaded. "Just watch after Linell and Latrell and make sure that they safe. I'm not sure how all this is gonna play out tonight, but I'm tired of runnin' already, I'm tired of hidin'. I'mma have to do something."

Chapter 13

Kayla had never been as nervous as she was when she was riding in the back of Juan's car. Up in the front passenger seat was Brandon while Kayla sat next to Marcus in the back seat. The streets of Indianapolis felt eerie to everyone that night, as the car followed Roy, who was a good block or so ahead. As they headed out of the more urbanized areas of the city and into the winding sloping northwest neighborhood that hugged Cold Springs Road, Kayla was somewhat in disbelief about it all.

"You okay?" Marcus asked, looking over at his woman. He could tell that she was deep in her feeling. "Kayla?"

Kayla leaned over, resting her head on Marcus' good shoulder. "Yeah, I'm okay I guess," she answered. "I was just thinkin' about some of what my mama was saying to me on the phone before I basically had to hang up on her."

"When you went outside?" Marcus asked, wanting clarification. "What did she say? That she didn't want you to go with us and take this nigga out?"

Kayla nodded. "Yup," she said. "Basically, that's what she said to me. She made it very clear that she didn't think I should go and that I should just let you all handle it and go on and do whatever you were going to do. I told her I felt her on what she was saying, but with a bullet in my little sister, this was starting to feel a little personal to me too. This Hakim dude shot my man, had people come over to my house and hold my family hostage, then gon' come back and shoot up my Godmother's house. That shit ain't gon fly with me. I don't care if me and you just sittin' in this car while they go in and get him." Kayla shook her head. "I feel good just bein' here."

Kayla patted the gun that was in her pocket. Since she was not given one of the guns that had a silencer, she instead had to carry a regular gun – a gun that made noise. Her job was to chill in the car with Marcus while Roy and Brandon and

Juan went in and handled business. However, if either of them saw a car heading up toward Hakim's property, they were to fire one shot in the air. This one shot would tell Juan and Brandon and Roy that somebody was coming, and that they needed to be on full alert.

"We almost there," Juan said, seeing the road ahead of them wind and get incredibly dark. "Roy said that shit was up in some wooded area." He looked around, looking at how nice the houses were. "I ain't never been up and around here before," he added. "That nigga Hakim must really have some money. I mean, the nigga loaded."

"If he got niggas workin' for him while he just chillin' at home plottin'," Brandon said, "then I bet the nigga do got some money."

Soon enough, Juan was pulling the car into a driveway on a quiet street.

"Damn," Juan said. "This shit look like some shit in the movies. Look how far apart the houses are. And all the trees and shit around here."

"That's what Roy was sayin' was gonna work in our favor," Brandon pointed out.

When both cars had pulled into the driveway of a colonial-style home that was obviously empty, they turned their lights off at the same moment. Roy got out of the car and walked back to them. He leaned over, sticking his head into Juan's front window.

"Remember what I told y'all two niggas," Roy said, sounding very authoritative. "Y'all gon get in through the front, since you younger and shit and can handle that fence." He then pointed toward the backyard of the house in front of them. "I'mma go back there and walk along the edge, or just inside, of the wooded area back there. Only a couple houses down to get to Hakim' house. Like I said back at the house, I'mma go in through the back while y'all causin' a bit of a commotion at the front. Remember, don't step out in the light, or outside of the wooded area of his yard until y'all done shot into the nigga's house so much that it done made the nigga piss on himself."

Everyone in the car snickered but Roy was being serious. Something deep down in his gut told him that his sister Lorna was inside of that house. He didn't even need to be reassured of that. When he was over there just yesterday, he got a strong vibe that this house, on Cold Springs Road, was probably the main house that Hakim used and stayed at in the city while he had smaller, poorer-type houses that were located in different hoods, spread about.

"A'ight," Juan said, pushing his car door open. "We got you, Roy. We got you."

"Okay," Roy said. He then moved back to Marcus' window. "Marcus, I know you wanna get up and do some shit. I get that and I really do understand, but just try to remember that y'all two need to just sit out in the car until you see us comin' out. Juan gon' leave the keys with you in case somethin' happen. And, make sure you watchin' out for cars. Keep your heads down low so these white people who might be ridin' by won't see a couple niggas in a car that is parked in front of a house that ain't even supposed to be havin' anybody livin' in it."

At the same time, Marcus and Kayla said "okay" and agreed with the orders. Roy leaned down and looked across the backseat to Kayla.

"And Kayla," Roy said. "I'mma need you to be brave," he told her. "I'mma need for you to really be watchin'. I want you to fire that gun one time in the air, while the two of y'all leanin' down, and with your hand outside of the window, of course, if you see anybody that look like they try'na come into Hakim's front gate down there." He pointed down the street. "Okay?"

Kayla nodded, willing to do whatever she needed to do so that she and her family would be safe again. "Okay," she said.

"A'ight," Roy said, leaning back up. "Let's go."

Kayla and Marcus watched as Juan and Brandon walked along the front yards of the neighboring houses, eventually disappearing into the darkness that engulfed the road further down. Roy, on the other hand, walked around and behind the vacant home. They watched his head go up and down until he was out of sight, swallowed up by darkness.

"This some scary shit, ain't it?" Marcus said, out loud, not even really addressing Kayla.

Kayla nodded her head, wondering all the time if she'd even made the right choice by coming along. "Yeah," she responded. "It's so dark over here."

***

Inside, Hakim was having what could only be described as a good old time with Amber. She stripped for him in his family room. All the while, Hakim's eyes were glued to how her ass was clapping. It even sounded big and fat by how her cheeks were clapping together, making a heavy sound.

"Shake that shit, bitch!" Hakim told her. He reached out, putting his drink down onto the coffee table before pressing his face into Amber's backside. "Damn this shit is fat," he told her.

Amber, as usual, used Hakim's comments as motivation. She shook her ass like her life depended on it, knowing that she would probably get a little bit of a shopping spree tomorrow if she could get Hakim in the mood.

While Hakim was upstairs with his chick, Jayrone and Raul were downstairs. The two were flipping back and forth through some sports channels, watching the world go by, so to speak.

"Why that nigga have us over here just to tease us?" Jayrone said, clearly annoyed. For the better part of the last half hour or so, they had been able to hear Hakim upstairs with Amber.

"Nigga, I told you," Raul said to Jayrone. "He want us to stay over here cause he know that nigga Marcus gon' come poppin' up." Just then, Raul pointed at the spare bedroom door. They both knew that behind it was Lorna's thick, naked body.

"I know, I know," Jayrone said. "This shit just don't feel right. I mean, look what the fuck we doin'. We sittin' down here, in the fuckin' basement, watchin' whatever sports game is on until the next commercial comes in, cutting us off. What the fuck is Hakim' doin? Upstairs with some bitch, playin' music and shit, probably about to get some of the best damn pussy. This shit is fucked up."

"So, what you sayin'?" Raul asked. "You sayin' you wanna go fuck that bitch, the nigga's mama?"

Jayrone looked at Raul and shook his head. "Naw," he said. "Nigga, you crazy. You know what Hakim would do if he found out."

"If..." Raul said, smiling. "If is the key word, my nigga. If he finds out. Who the fuck say he got to know?"

Jayrone looked at Raul with a confused look. "What the fuck you mean, Raul?" he asked. "What the fuck you talkin' bout?"

"Look, nigga," Raul said, tapping Jayrone's arm and looking back toward the staircase leading upstairs. "Like you said, that nigga bout to be deep in the pussy. If that's the case, then why the fuck would he even be worried about what's goin' on down here. Hell, that bitch in that room could scream from the dick that we givin' her and he still wouldn't hear anything."

"You think we should?" Jayrone asked, feeling himself get a hard-on. "I mean, for real though," he said, "You not gon' tell Hakim, is you?"

"Tell Hakim?" Raul asked, almost feeling as if he were being insulted. "Nigga, you know damn well I ain't gon tell Hakim shit." He looked back toward the basement steps and lowered his voice, leaning in toward Jayrone. "I just want some of that pussy in there," he said. "And Hakim ain't got shit he gotta say about it. For real, though. We coulda just took the bitch's pussy at her house."

Jayrone smiled. "That's what we shoulda did," he said. "But then Hakim might'a felt them sloppy seconds we would leave his ass. You know what the chicks out in the streets be sayin' about that nigga. They say his dick little."

Jayrone and Raul broke into laughter. Within a couple of minutes, they both were rising up off of the couch. As they moved toward the room where Lorna was being held, Jayrone noticed something move out in the front yard. With the basement windows to the front being behind them, neither of them had spent much time looking out of them. Jayrone tapped Raul's arm quickly. He pointed at the window.

"What?" Raul asked.

"Look out front," Jayrone said.

Just then, Raul looked toward the basement step. It became very clear that someone was walking in the front yard. At first, Raul had begun to wonder why neither one of them had heard the dog, Roxy, barking. Then, he remembered that Roxy was out in the backyard and probably didn't hear whatever could be happening out front.

"You see that shit?" Jayrone asked. "You see that shit, nigga?"

Raul nodded. "Hell yeah," he said. "Look like somebody out in the front yard."

Quickly, the two of them grabbed their guns off of the basement coffee table and turned the television down. Just as they were heading toward the basement steps, having forgotten all about Lorna and what they were going to do to her, a popping noise began. First, one of the basement windows broke. Then another. At this point, the two of them had ducked behind the couch. They knew that whoever was shooting at Hakim's house had silencers on their guns. That would make it all the more dangerous. Amber's screams then seeped down the steps, telling them that something bad was really about to happen.

***

Roy walked along the edge of the adjoining back yard, slowly moving toward Hakim's house. He felt as if God was looking down on him by giving him so much dark, wooded land to work with. He walked just inside of the wood's edge until he came up to where Hakim's property started. He took a moment to look up at the house before realizing that a Pit Bull was running straight at him, seeming to come from the middle of the yard. Before Roy knew it, the dog was barking and growling and practically up to his shit. Quickly, not wanting to get bit and definitely not wanting the dog to draw any more attention to him than it had already done, Roy raised his gun up and fired. The dog yelped once as it fell into the snow.

"Sorry, doggy," Roy said, sarcastically. "Everybody gotta die tonight."

Once Roy checked his surroundings and was sure that nobody was coming out of the back of their house and toward him, he inched out into the backyard. For the next several yards, he felt so exposed. There he was, tall and dressed in dark coloring, making his way across a snow-covered yard that was lit up by the moon.

As Roy got closer to the basement of the house, which let out to a patio that was surrounded by what appeared to be dead rose bushes, he ducked down. He hurried up and hid behind the cluster of bushes. Once there, he could see inside. It became very clear, very quickly that Juan and Brandon had already begun to shoot into Hakim's house. He could see two dudes, one who clearly had some Hispanic blood in him, ducking down behind the couch and looking over the edge. These guys looked just like who Kayla had seen.

Roy sat there, kneeling and waiting for his chance. He knew that since Brandon and Juan had begun to shoot into the house, it would only be a matter of time before whoever these two dudes were went running up the steps. While standing there, Roy could see that they were carrying guns. This left no doubt in Roy's mind that these two dudes were Hakim's boys – boys he would send to do his dirty work for him. *You'll get yours soon enough*, Roy thought to himself. "Oh yeah," he said, the words practically slipping out of his mouth.

Roy waited and waited, wondering what was taking the two guys so long to head up the stairs. Within a minute or so, they rushed from behind the couch and headed upstairs. Roy knew that this was his chance – his opportunity to run up into the house. Quickly, he came from around the desolate bushes and up to the French doors that let out of the basement and onto the brick patio. After looking inside, he stepped back a few feet once he was sure that nobody else appeared to be waiting down in the basement. Only using one bullet, he shot out the small glass that was above and to the left of the door handle. Once the glass hit the floor, he reached in, moving ever so smoothly, and unlocked the French door.

Once Roy pushed the door open, seeing the television on and clear evidence that two men had been sitting on the couch that was in front of him, he stepped inside. He could hear commotion going on upstairs. There was no doubt that the commotion was Hakim and his boys jumping into action.

Roy walked ahead toward the steps, watching every which way that he could, and constantly checking behind him. He checked inside of a doorway off to the side, finding that it was empty. He then checked another door, finding that it led to a very nicely designed and decorated bathroom. Finally, he only had one door left, which was on the other side of the room. He guessed that there might be a bedroom down in this basement since the bathroom was built with a full bathtub and shower.

Roy approached the door and then stopped, noticing that it locked from the outside, which made him pause. *What kinda door would be locked from the outside?*

Roy answered his own question: A door that you wouldn't want anyone to get out of. For whatever reason, his gut told him that his sister Lorna could be in this room. It only made sense.

Carefully, as to not make too much noise, Roy approached the door. He lightly tapped on it.

"Lorna?" Roy said, softly. "Lorna? Are you in there?"

"Roy?" Lorna said, clearly sounding as if notes of joy had taken over her voice. "Roy, is that you?"

Without a second thought, Roy fidgeted with the lock until the door open. Once his eyes took in the fact that the room was a spare bedroom, he stepped inside. He found his sister Lorna, on a bed, wrapped up in a sheet.

"What happened to you?" Roy asked, watching as Lorna stood up, holding the sheet around her body.

"You gotta get me outta here," Lorna said. "Before that nigga come back down again and rape me."

"Rape you?" Roy said, instantly becoming enraged. "Did that nigga rape you, Lorna? Did that nigga rape you?"

Lorna hesitated, feeling ashamed that she wasn't strong enough to fight off being taken out of her house, let alone actually being raped in Hakim's house. She nodded. "Where am I, Roy? Where the fuck am I?"

Roy told his younger sister to be quiet as he guided her out of the room.

"Find your clothes," he told her. "They must'a done something with them. They probably down here somewhere. Whatever you do, don't make a lot of noise. Find your shit and get it on and hide, somewhere. Just stay out of sight. If you can, run out into the yard and hide on the side of the house or somethin'."

"And where you goin'?" Lorna asked, looking very concerned.

Roy pointed toward the stairs. "I'm goin' up them steps right there," he answered. "I came here to kill this nigga, even if it kills me. You just get your clothes and worry about hiding. I don't know how much shit is about to pop off over here, so you just get out of dodge as best as you can."

Lorna did just as she was told, rushing passed her brother. Roy then headed toward the steps and began to slowly climb them. He didn't know what he was going to find upstairs. However, he was sure glad that the element of surprise was working in his favor. It became very clear that whomever was upstairs had no idea that he was coming up.

***

"These niggas wanna play games and shit with me, huh?" Hakim asked, having pushed Amber to go hide in the kitchen.

When Raul and Jayrone came up the steps after the silent bullets came rushing into the house, they had their guns already out. Quickly, being prepared as he always was, Hakim went to his secret hiding spot—the refrigerator. Now that he was packing some heat – heat that was more powerful than your average handgun – he turned off all of the lights on that floor. Right along with Raul and Jayrone, they shot out into the front yard, randomly.

"Damn, Hakim," Raul said. "We can't even see where we shootin'!"

"That don't matter," Hakim said, firing another round into his dark front yard. "Don't give a fuck about all that. Just shoot at these niggas," he told them.

Following orders, and not caring that the neighborhood lit up with loud gunshots, all three of them fired into the front yard. At first, Jayrone thought that he'd seen somebody move to his left. He fired over there. Then, Raul thought that he'd seen someone moving to his right. He fired over there. Hakim, who stood in the middle, watched his yard very closely. Just as he was about to fire again, he heard Amber yell. This caused all three of them to turn around, quickly and look around the dark house.

"What the fuck she yellin' for?" Hakim said. "What the fuck that bitch yellin' for?"

Just then, on both sides of Hakim, Raul fell, then Jayrone. They both had been shot by one of the silent bullets – bullets that appeared to be coming out of the dark. For the first time in years, Hakim could feel himself getting a little scared. Before he knew it, Amber was being pushed into the little bit of light that was shining from the moon, into the middle of the living room floor. That was when, right then and there, that his eyes met with Roy's eyes. Hakim grinned, watching Roy hold Amber at gunpoint.

"Well, ain't this somethin'?" Roy said sarcastically as Amber squirmed in his arms. "Look like pussy got you by the tongue, huh?"

Hakim shook his head. "You really went through all this to save that little nigga? Huh, Roy? Nigga, you know this shit wasn't even worth it. He just gon' fuck up again and do somethin' that get you killed."

"And my sister?" Roy asked. "You was down there rapin' her."

Hakim looked toward the basement steps, realizing that he'd fallen for the diversion that was all set up for him to be surprised. He laughed. "Yep," he said. "And damn, nigga, she got that good pussy, even if I do say so myself."

Roy pressed the barrel of his gun harder into the side of Amber's head.

Hakim chuckled. "You think I care about that bitch?" he lifted his gun up and pointed it at Amber. "I couldn't care less if you kill that bitch. She ain't nothin' but a ass and some lips to me."

"Please," Amber said. "Please don't kill me. Hakim, make him stop. Make him stop, Hakim."

Hakim showed no remorse for Amber and how she was being held hostage. At this point, all he really cared about was getting himself out alive. And he was willing to let her die for that to happen. He could get another bitch to replace her, any day of the week.

"Nigga, you done really fucked up too much at this point," Roy said. "You done fucked with my family and kidnapped my sister while making Marcus's girlfriend Kayla's life a living hell. Nigga, I came here to kill you, not negotiate with you."

No sooner than Hakim could move his lips to form a smirk, Roy had turned his gun toward Hakim. He fired, leaving Amber to watch as Hakim's body fell to the ground. Roy watched as the chick rushed over to Hakim – rushed over to the very dude that had basically just given him the okay to kill her.

Roy raised his gun at the chick's head as his own head was shaking side to side. "Bitch, you gon' die too," he said.

Just as Amber turned around, with a look of terror, her eyes met with Roy's eyes, and she knew it was too late. Roy pulled the trigger and listened to the ping, watching as Amber sloped down and on top of Hakim's body. Roy stood there for a moment, looking at all four dead bodies, knowing that what he'd just done was completely necessary.

Sirens rung into the air. The plan was that if they heard police sirens, no matter how far away they seemed, Juan and Brandon needed to rush back down the block to the car. Roy could only hope that the two of them were doing just that as he rushed downstairs, grabbed his sister, and the two of them darted across the backyard. Roy guided her along the edges of the woods and down a couple of houses until they dashed across that backyard. Once they came up to the driveway of the empty house, Marcus was grateful to be reunited with his mother. They all climbed into their cars, with Lorna getting into the car with Roy, and sat there for a moment. Police cars rushed down the block, causing all of them to duck down a little bit. As they looked down the block, watching cops bowguard through Hakim's gate and up his driveway, they knew that the worst part was over. They waited until no more police cars pulled up before very casually pulling out of the driveway and heading back down the street in the opposite direction.

Chapter 14

Kayla and Marcus were able to pick up right where they left off with their relationship. That night, after running in on Hakim and his boys, they took the long way back to Roy's house. Just in case any neighbor had given the police descriptions of two cars pulling off, they would have a hell of a time finding those two cars.

Marcus talked with everyone involved, getting them to agree that Kayla just didn't need to know about what happened between him and Tweety. In fact, Marcus wanted to carry that to the grave. He knew that his guilt would only intensify if Kayla knew that another woman was behind Hakim's rage. In fact, Marcus was more than sure that Tweety was probably the one who took part of the brick then blamed it on him.

Kayla, with her secret situation with Jonathon, actually was called in to interview for the job at the library. Upon getting the job, Jonathon persisted with trying to get in her pants. Kayla refused, knowing that he really wasn't helping her, but rather, was just doing what he could to get a little arrangement going with a sexy chick.

Linell made a full recovery from being shot. The nine-year old was stronger than anyone believed. The doctors were actually able to save her kidney, which had been punctured by the bullet. The little girl would only have to go through several months of rehabilitation and testing, to be sure that her organ functioned properly.

Kayla learned a lot about trust over these few days of her life. She also learned how quickly something can turn sour, even when you are least expecting it. Marcus didn't trust his boys enough to even tell them that he was going down to Texas, let alone that he had Hakim after him. Lorna didn't trust Brandon and Juan any further than she could throw them. This at least changed, however, once she got back to the car that night outside of Hakim's place and saw that they'd come through to help save her son. Kayla hoped to God that Marcus never found about what she'd done for Jonathon. If Marcus was going to clean up his life, she wanted to be sure that he was doing it with someone he could trust.

CPSIA information can be obtained
at www.ICGtesting.com
Printed in the USA
LVOW13s1822210917
549566LV00011B/1000/P